The Hate Crime

JOHN A. RUSSO

Burning Bulb
PUBLISHING

The Hate Crime
by **John A. Russo**

Burning Bulb Publishing
P.O. Box 4721
Bridgeport, WV 26330-4721
www.BurningBulbPublishing.com

Cover designed by Gary Lee Vincent.

Paperback edition ISBN: 978-1-964172-29-3

CHAPTER 1

By now virtually everybody knows me not just for my horror-movie franchise, *Intensive Scare Parts One, Two, Three* and so on, but also for writing a book called *The Killing Truth* about the first murder that Vito Martinelli and I solved, a cold case concerning the murder of my best friend, Ronald Demick, when we were thirteen years old. After that, Vito and I teamed up, along with my daughter Joy, then twenty-six years old, to solve a second case. I wrote about that one in yet another best-seller, titled *The Killer and the Movie Star.*

In spite of my commercial successes, or because of them, I was pigeonholed when it came to making "serious" movies or writing "serious" books, even though in the privacy of my mind I considered myself sort of a Renaissance Man, deeply interested in everything going on in the world. So I took the leap and wrote a novel called *Dealey Plaza* which was a reflection on the decades-old epidemic of mass violence that began with the Kennedy assassination. I pressured the publisher of my genre novels into putting it out, and nobody took much notice of it. I think as soon as reviewers saw my name on the book, they dismissed it, maybe even dumped it in a Goodwill bin. I had to swallow the fact that my effort to create something "important" did not succeed.

However, my morale got a bit of a boost in June of 2003 when a much-cherished old friend phoned me out of the blue and told me how much he loved *Dealey Plaza*, which I considered my finest work. I would've been glad to hear from him even if he hated it because we had been so close. I laughed when he said,

"Your movie tie-in novels are pretty much crap, but I really loved this one called *Dealey Plaza* and you should do more of them."

"I'd very much like to," I informed him, "but it sold less than five thousand copies."

"Too bad," he said. "Maybe it's because most people don't read anymore and they don't ev know where Dealey Plaza is. But that's not the main reason I called you."

"Well, thanks for reading it," I said. "I'd love to see you."

The two of us were great pals all the way into our twenties, but I hadn't seen or heard from him for about twenty years. His name was Roland Fornier, pronounced Fornyay because it was French. Back when we were teenagers, Roland was considered a black sheep. Most parents didn't allow their kids to hang out with him. He got called "that jailbird's son" due to the fact his father, who used to be a councilman, had tried to defraud the city of Clairton on a bogus land deal and got sentenced to three years behind bars.

My father, who was a brutal alcoholic, treated Roland much better than he treated me and my mother. He let Roland hang out at our house, joked with him man to man and even sometimes let him eat dinner with us. Roland loved spaghetti and meatballs, and nobody made it better than my mom did. I think Roland's "bad boy" reputation appealed to my father's dark side. Roland and I used to get into wacky things that were different from the kinds of things I got into with Ron Demick, who was timid and self-effacing while Roland was brash—to put it mildly. The off-the-wall Don Martin cartoons in *Mad Magazine* made us laugh till our sides hurt. We got off on the way the editors shot down the angry prudes who called the magazine demented, malicious, or just plain obnoxious. Their standard reply was "*We don't care what you think of us as long as you plunked down your twenty-five cents.*" When either Roland or I got our hands on a new issue, we would opt out of pick-up baseball games and stand on

4

the sidelines yucking it up and passing it back and forth, reading over each other's shoulders.

Around the time I turned sixteen, Roland started teaching me how to box. I was only five-eight and one hundred and forty pounds, but he was a big, strapping, rawboned fellow with a hot temper and an ingrained meanness when he felt he was wronged, qualities that made a gym owner take him under his wing and coach him into contending for the Golden Gloves and then turning him into a professional heavyweight. In the meantime, my dad, probably not wanting me to be a sissy or, worse, gay, had bought me a punching bag and a pair of boxing gloves for my twelfth birthday, but I had never used them, and when Roland found out he said, "I'm gonna teach you all the stuff I'm learning at Cherry Red's. We're gonna build ourselves a boxing ring."

So, we went into the woods behind my street and dug post holes and chopped down trees to make ring posts. Then we stole bull ropes from coal barges on the Monongahela River and dragged them up through the woods and made them into ring ropes. Our ring was in a clearing in the peach orchard behind a little store in an alley. The gloves my dad had bought me were too small for Roland, but he forced his big hands into them when he sparred with me, teaching me to jab straight and bring the punches straight back to my shoulder, to never take roundhouse swings that would leave me to open to a counterpunch, and to get inside and go for the opponent's belly and solar plexus in order to wear him down. I became pretty good at it, and Roland and I started coaxing kids we didn't like to get in the ring with us so we could kick their asses. But I got my comeuppance when I instigated a fight with a boy I didn't like because he was always picked to play quarterback in our pickup games, only because he was tall, and not because he was really any good at throwing passes, especially deep ones. He was a foot taller than me and had a much longer reach. I was trying to get inside and work his body when he hit me with a long-armed jab that damn near broken my nose. I was gushing blood, so I had to quit, utterly humiliated. I couldn't "throw in the towel" because I was profusely bleeding into it.

Later on, when I was in basic training at Fort Jackson, South Carolina, I entered the boxing ring against a recruit named Pete Bragg, who was considered the best middleweight in the battalion, and I used the things I had learned from Roland to win a decision. After that, some of the rednecks who had ridiculed me as a namby-pamby college boy stopped ragging on me. They would say, "Tell the truth—you're Golden Gloves," and I didn't confirm or deny because I wanted to keep them a little scared of me.

I had volunteered to enter the Army as a draftee soon after I graduated from college, wanting to get my military service over with in only two years so I could plunge into writing and filmmaking. Roland did four years as an enlisted man. In high school he had given up boxing to play football and made All State guard on our state champion football team, but he gave up college scholarships to go into the Army. He became an airborne MP stationed at Fort Bragg, then he was sent to Germany. I served almost all of my two years at that same post, but my time didn't overlap Roland's, and I got out ahead of him. After he was discharged, he became a car salesman while I was trying to be a filmmaker, not getting hired anywhere and trying to make it on my own, and both of us needed to live with our parents because we couldn't afford to share an apartment. But at least his family situation had improved because his father had done his time and was out of prison.

Roland and I went on a few double dates, but that routine didn't last long. I was baffled and amazed when he up and married a bleach-bottle-blonde who was only sixteen years old. "She's beautiful, isn't she?" he asked me, and I had to agree even though I didn't think so. But he fell hard and moved in with her.

6

Then he disappeared from my life for a couple of years and when I next saw him, he was going through a divorce and a custody battle. He was also selling cemetery plots instead of cars. Now and then he would barge into one of the millworker bars in our old hometown wearing a three-piece suit with little spade shovels for cufflinks and a tie clasp, and would laugh his head off chasing young barflies around with a measuring tape, pretending he was measuring them up for their coffins.

In the late 1970s on one of his spur-of-the-moment appearances in town, he got into a fistfight with George Kosana, a formidable bar brawler endowed with a measure of local fame for playing the sheriff in *Night of the Living Dead*. We called him "Kus." Somehow, he had gotten in with one of George Romero's partners and had helped wrangle zombies and posse members, then got typecast. The famous fight between him and Roland happened at the Clairton VFW, which used to have a huge picture window in front but now had a very small one, because they crashed through it and then back through it and sent liquor bottles crashing and shattering, like a brawl in a Western movie. Police sirens wailed, and they ran through shards of glass and both of them jumped into Roland's car because Kus had come there with someone else. Roland peeled out, both of them laughing like hell and becoming buddies. They never got arrested, probably because of the code of silence that prevailed in all the rough and tough mill towns in the valley.

Around that same time, a few scenes from *The Deer Hunter* were filmed in Clairton before the production moved to Mingo Junction, Ohio, because the director needed vistas of blast-furnaces and thick roiling smoke in the backgrounds of the mill workers' houses, and those kinds of vistas weren't possible in the lower part of Clairton where the coke works was located. The performances of the actors playing zany tough-guy mill workers was applauded by critics and fans, but I knew that the real-life characters were actually a lot zanier and more authentic.

I had written a script that would have proven me correct, and I was miffed that I probably would never get it green-lighted.

After his brawl with Kus, it was a while before Roland dared to come back into town and barge into his favorite local bar with his spade cufflinks, tie clasp, and tape measure. On one of those times, I met up with him. He had put on about twenty or thirty pounds, but he was still craggily handsome and deeply tanned, and he told me he had been living in Florida after getting cut from the Philadelphia Eagles, who had given him a tryout. We drank together till the wee hours, and he informed me, with a laugh and a smirk, that he had been hanging out in Miami with Chicago mob boss Sam Giancana and Sam's girlfriend, one of the famous Andrews Sisters, who had had a string of hit songs on the top forty. Not long after I learned that Roland knew Sam Giancana. Sam was shot in the face in his own home with a .22 caliber pistol, a typical weapon used by mob assassins, and there was a rumor that he had helped mastermind the Kennedy assassination in cahoots with Carlos Marcello, his mob counterpart in New Orleans, who had him bumped off in order to silence him.

I was streetwise enough not to bring subjects of that sort up with Roland. There were rumors he had become a hitman, and I half believed them. He was so circumspect about his activities and his whereabouts I never knew when he would show up. When he did show up, I never asked him how his divorce and custody battle had turned out or anything else that might hit him the wrong way. On one of those off-the-cuff-type occasions we got drunk together and joked about old times. I asked him what it had been like fighting Kus, and he said it was like trying to grapple with a three-hundred-pound bowling ball.

After that visit, I didn't see or hear from him again for about twenty years, till the day he phoned and told me how much he liked *Dealey Plaza*. When I said I would love to see him, he said, "That's what I'm really calling about." He told me he was driving to Clairton from somewhere, but he didn't say where, only that he wanted to meet me at a bar that used to serve us beer and wine when we were teenagers. Back then it was called The Hideaway but now it was called The Interchange. When I went in, I found that it pretty much looked the same except that the red leatherette upholstery on the booths was old and cracked with some of the stuffing leaking out.

I was wearing Levis and a black T-shirt with one of my movie posters silk-screened onto it, and Roland was wearing black trousers and a black belt with a silver rodeo buckle and a green shirt with epaulettes; its short sleeves enabling me to see that his biceps were as big and hard as ever. His hair was as gray as mine, though. I was clean-shaven while he sported a neat gray mustache. We ordered shots of VO Gold with beer chasers, and he started speaking his mind even before the waitress brought the drinks to our booth.

"I'm going to fill you in on what I've been into for a long time," he said, "but you better not tell a soul."

What a difference twenty or so years make. He had never before talked to me like that, and I was taken aback. I blinked and shrugged but said nothing.

"I'm taking a big chance," he said. "I hope I can trust you. If you agree to do what I want, you don't confide in anyone but Vito Martinelli. You hear me?"

"What about my daughter, Joy? She works for him now."

"She's trustworthy?"

"Absolutely. Otherwise, they'd be out of business."

"I'll take your word for it, but if the shit hits the fan, it's on you."

I let that slide and waited for him to open up. We downed a couple more shots of VO Gold. Then he said, "I had to go on the lam and make myself scarce for damn near twenty years. If you remember, I was going through a messy divorce and a custody battle when we were in our twenties. Well, I came home one day

9

and caught that bitch in the bathroom with my daughter, Stephanie, and she was about to slit Stephanie's throat."

"Damn! Are you serious?"

"Serious as brain cancer." He chugged some beer and slammed his bottle down. "I punched her in her fuckin' face and she went down, out cold. I should've grabbed the razor and slit *her* throat right then and there. But I got the hell out of there, both me and Stephanie, and took off because I knew she'd get the US Marshals after us. That lyin' piece of shit put on an act that fooled everybody into thinking she was Miss Goody Two Shoes—that's how she got custody. So I had to go into hiding and keep my kid safe till she turned eighteen, because by then my ex-wife couldn't take her back if she didn't want to be taken. Which she wouldn't because she hated that bitch's guts. But the fucking court system was on her side. The law came after *me*, goddamn it! And she got money from her father to hire a couple of private detectives. They found out where we were and they tried to kidnap Stephanie one day when she was on her way to school and she smashed one of them in the face with her lunch bucket and got away. But we were forced to go on the run again."

"Where to?" I asked.

"Don't ask," Roland said. "Too many places to remember. We had to hide, but I always tried to make things as normal as possible for Stephanie. I had to keep getting her used to one fake name after another just to put her in schools. I always bought her expertly forged birth certificates. We hid for a couple years on a farm near Gettysburg." He grinned and suppressed a laugh. "One day I was so drunk I took a shortcut through the Gettysburg Battlefield, which is illegal, and I didn't want any cops to spot me so I dimmed my headlights and crashed head on into one of the Civil War statues." He chuckled wryly. "I told the cops I didn't have a choice when that Union soldier charged me with his bayonet, but they didn't think that was funny, and they put the cuffs on me. Luckily my driver's license was a very good forgery. But I had to pay somebody off so I didn't go to jail."

I said, Now that Stephanie is way past eighteen.""Yeah, but now I've got a worse problem."

"Uh oh. I guess I was afraid of that."

"Yeah, Dave, it never ends. I try to remember that life is an unending series of problems and all we can do is deal with them, but when do I get any peace, or at least some normality? I thought I was doing a good job of raising Stephanie in spite of having to be on the run all the time, but I didn't know she was getting into some bad shit behind my back. She got pregnant by a classmate of hers while we were living in the Gettysburg area. A pimple-faced kid, for chrissake! I didn't want her to marry him. But she didn't want to give the baby up for adoption, which is what I advised her to do. She gave birth when she was only fifteen, but there were severe complications, and she didn't make it. She left me with a grandchild. A baby girl."

"What's her name?" I asked, just to slow things up because he was hitting me with so much new stuff, and most of it not so lovely. And I sensed that there might be worse to come. Answering my question about his grandchild's name, he said, "Katherine. I knew that's what Stephanie had intended to name her, so I respected that and followed through. For the next dozen years or so, I thought she was a success story because she was on the Honor Roll no matter what school I had to put her into, but I couldn't always keep tabs on her because I was on the road too much selling hot water heaters and other stuff, even slot machines to the Native American tribes that operate casinos. She got in with the skinhead crowd when she was a freshman in high school. It damn near tore my heart out. We had relocated for the umpteenth time and were living on the outskirts of Charlotte, North Carolina, and unbeknownst to me, she fell under the spell of a fucked-up pervert named Kirk Biggins, a recruiter and bomb maker for a bunch of neo-Nazi fanatics who call themselves the

Aryan Confederacy. His MO was to lurk around high schools, trying to turn teenage boys into skinheads and girls into sex slaves."

He waited while the waitress put another round of drinks in front of us, then went on. "Katherine was easy prey for the wily sonofabitch. I grounded her to keep her away from that asshole. I said I'd nail the windows shut if I had to, and she threatened to run away with him. I knew I couldn't watch her *all* the time; I had to earn a living. I was still working under the table jobs where I wouldn't need a legit social security card or driver's license. I was scared my shady past might catch up with me."

It occurred to me that doing hits might have been one of the under the table jobs he had resorted to, but I still didn't want to believe those rumors were true.

He said, "The best thing that could've happened was if Biggins would've blown himself up with one of his own bombs. But no such luck. He manipulated Katherine into playing hooky so he could get her to a J.P. and marry her. The sonofabitch had more legal status than I did after that. He started isolating her and beating the hell out of her if she didn't give him exactly what he wanted, including some nasty, ugly S&M things. He threatened to let his skinhead plug-uglies gangbang her if she tried to get away from him."

"How do you know all that?" I asked him.

He took a deep breath and looked totally glum. Then he said, "Katherine knew she'd have to kill Kirk Biggins or he'd never let her go. So that's what she ended up doing. Shot him in their bed. But she didn't get away. Instead, she was arrested almost immediately. I found out most of the stuff I just told you because it was part of her testimony at trial. I had no contact with her after she ran off with Biggins. I didn't even know till she was arrested that *she* had daughter, five years old at the time of her trial, in January 2003The kid was named Magda because Biggins wanted her to have a Kraut-sounding name. When

Katherine testified on her own behalf, she claimed she had killed Biggins not only for beating her constantly and threatening to kill her, but because he had a prior conviction for molesting little boys and was on the verge of doing the same thing to Magda."

"Damn!" I said. "What a cross to carry! But you seem to be holding up so well."

"On the outside, not always on the inside," Roland said wryly.

"Tell me something. Is this the case that was tried in Boston? Because we all read about it. Me and Roland and Joy."

"Yeah, you're right, Dave. Katherine killed Biggins in Boston. He wanted to explode his first dirty bomb there in hopes of starting a second American revolution. The FBI and the ATF found plans and partially assembled devices in his garage. Thousands and maybe millions of people would've died if Katherine hadn't shot Kirk Biggins in his bed with his own Luger. It was clear that she had done the world a favor. She had to be put on trial, but the prosecutors made her a deal that didn't include a prison sentence, instead they would put her into the Witness Protection Program. The last I saw of her was when she was handcuffed and dragged out of the courtroom to I don't know where."

I said, "I'd be going bonkers if it was my own daughter. I'd beat the shit out of anybody who knew anything till they coughed it up."

"Yeah, but I'm stumped," Roland said dolefully. "Katherine isn't in Witness Protection any longer, and I don't know why. She stayed in it for less than a year. Then she just left, just this past March, taking Magda with her. Homeland Security grilled me about her whereabouts, scarcely mentioning Magda, but I think I convinced them I don't have a clue. They want to locate Katherine in case she knows more about the dirty bombs than she admitted. Just because she killed her fucked-up husband it doesn't mean she wasn't working side by side with him, aiding and abetting."

"Yeah, that's the way they would think," I said.

"I need to find her. I have to know whether she's alive or dead. Biggins's cronies might be hunting her down in case she might know how to get in touch with whoever was going to supply him with degraded uranium. I'm scared they'll torture her and then kill her."

"What kind of leads do you have on the Aryan Confederacy?"

"Well," Roland said, drawing the word out heavily, almost like a sigh, "I need help when it comes to online research and pursuit—digital tracking and all that stuff is not my thing. I don't want to hook up with the police. They wouldn't listen to me anyway, and I have no way of knowing what Homeland Security is up to. I think they'd sacrifice Katherine if push came to shove—for the so-called good of the country."

"You might be right."

"Damn straight," he said. "So when are you gonna talk to Vito?"

"I'll head right over there," I told him.

CHAPTER 2

"Roland's granddaughter is Katherine Biggins," I informed Vito and Joy.

"Oh my god!" Joy blurted.

Vito, who was usually unfazed by almost anything, said, "Are you sure? She's the same gal who shot her abusive husband in his sleep?"

"One and the same," I acknowledged.

"And he was that neo-Nazi?"

"Uh-huh. Roland said he was glad she killed him."

"So am I," Joy stated adamantly.

Vito's office was in downtown Clairton, where I had grown up, a working man's city of about 20,000 people. He and Joy were seated around his conference table with burgers, fries, and Cokes in front of them, but they hadn't unwrapped any of it yet.

Joy said, "Want me to order something for you, Dad?"

"No, thanks," I said. "I want to tell you the rest of the situation, and it'll take a while."

I took a seat, anxious to get into the gist of my conversation with Roland. Vito and Joy kept munching while I talked. Then Joy stood up and said, "I'm going to Google everything I can find on Roland's daughter and print it out for you guys. We *are* going to take the case, aren't we, Vito?"

"Can't pass it up," he answered. "It takes something like this to get my blood flowing."

He was seventy-three years old but still in great shape, with the energy and drive of a much younger man. He was in jeans and a short-sleeved yellow shirt with black trim. His hair was still dark brown, and he claimed that he never dyed it, and I thought it might be true.

"If Katherine Biggins is still alive, I hope she kills more Nazis," Joy said

I admired her righteous anger and wanted to tell her how beautiful she looked, but she didn't trust compliments from her dad. She had shoulder-length ash-blonde hair and was wearing tan jeans, a pink blouse printed with flowers, tiny gold earrings, and a pendant on a thin gold chain. She balled up wrappers and leftover fries and tossed them into a wastebasket, then opened her laptop and started Googling.

Vito and I sat back and stared unseeingly at each other. I could guess that he must be as perplexed as I was, trying to deal with the realization that Roland's plight and the plight of his missing granddaughter were dilemmas much deeper and more complicated than anything we had dealt with up till now. Joy stood up and said, "Gotta get my printouts," and left the room.

"What does Roland want from us?" Vito asked me. "Let me hear it one more time."

"Find Katherine and Magda," I said. "Protect them if they aren't already dead. Report back to him as soon as we find out anything, especially if we bump shoulders with any of the Aryan Confederacy shitheads that might be after her."

"Sounds like he wants to take care of them on his own," Vito said. "And I guess I don't blame him. As long as none of the blowback hits us."

Joy came back into the conference room with a sheaf of printouts and handed each of us a copy of a newspaper article put out by the Southern Poverty Law Center a few weeks after Katherine was first arrested.

"Slain Neo-Nazi had 'Dirty Bomb' Components"

Kirk Biggins, the so-called "bomb master" of the domestic terrorist group that calls itself The Aryan Confederacy, was found to have a cache of materials and plans suitable for building a "dirty bomb." In his garage, ATF agents discovered containers filled with a mix of thorium and highly toxic beryllium powder plus a tank of a hydrogen-peroxide-based solution along with lithium, thermite, black iron oxide, and other substances used to amplify the effects of homemade explosives.

The Aryan Confederacy has been suspected of inciting mass shootings of minorities and the burning of churches and synagogues. Diminished in numbers currently, it once was one of the largest neo-Nazi militias in the United States.

Kirk Biggins was shot and killed by his wife, Katherine Biggins, who claimed that he violently abused her all during the five years of their marriage and was giving indications of doing the same to their four-year-old child, named Magda. Mrs. Biggins was given a suspended sentence and allowed to go free in a trial that some people believed to have ended in jury nullification. On her way to the acquittal, she took the stand and testified that she first put one of her husband's Lugers in her own mouth to commit suicide, but then decided she had to kill her husband to save herself and her toddler. The psychologist who evaluated her concluded that the turning point for her was Kirk Biggins's growing obsession with child pornography and her sense of "escalating doom."

During her trial, dozens of people picketed the courthouse every day, carrying FREE KATHERINE signs and banners.

The couples' bedroom was full of Nazi and White supremacist propaganda, including a large gold-framed photo of Timothy McVeigh, who was convicted and executed for detonating an ammonium nitrate and nitromethane fertilizer truck bomb in front of the Alfred P. Murrah Federal Building in Oklahoma City in 1995. The death toll from the blast was 168, many of them children.

Vito said, "This is some powerful shit, David. But how do we know that Roland's daughter isn't part of this Aryan

Confederacy outfit? If she isn't, why didn't she kill her husband sooner?"

"Good point," Joy said. "Any insights on that, Dad?"

"Well, I actually brought that up with Roland," I told them. "He said the prosecutors worked that angle really hard when she went on the stand. But they didn't rattle her. And the judge and jury believed her. Her bitterness against her dead husband was palpable. In fact she spat out that since he had specialized in committing hate crimes it was only fair that she had committed one against *him.*"

"Wow, poetic justice," Vito said. "She's my kind of gal."

I said, "Roland is staying at the Hampton Inn. He's not going to check out till he's told whether or not we're taking the case. I'll phone him and let him know and ask him to meet with us ASAP so we can pump him for more information. If he has any."

"Great. Let's go get a drink," said Vito.

In mill towns like Clairton, drinking was and still is a way of life. Most people weren't alcoholics like my dad was, but social occasions like weddings, funerals, Steelers games on TV at the American Legion, and most other gatherings involved alcohol. Vito grew up in that milieu the same as Roland and I did. But people didn't usually have bars in their homes. That's why when I started reading mystery novels by Raymond Chandler, Dashiel Hammett and others, it struck me odd that a lot of the passages involved a detective going into somebody's home or office to question him or her, and a drink would be offered first thing. Later I learned that those writers were alcoholics and so their thirst for alcohol seemed to get into their writing. I was reminded of this phenomenon in a slightly different way some years ago, when an actress asked me if I would critique her friend's screenplay, and after I read it I said, "He has too many scenes where people are eating. He has to think up some different things for them to do." And she laughed and said, "Well, he weighs four hundred pounds and he's always thinking about eating."I laughed and shook my head and never forgot that little insight.

CHAPTER 3

Almost immediately after abandoning the Witness Protection Program back in March of 2003 Katherine Biggins had procured forged documents under a new alias: Sarah Jamison. She had changed her appearance in case anyone was trying to hunt her down. She didn't think the authorities would, but with her late husband's cronies it might be a different story. When she had lived with him, she was a brunette and had kept her dark shoulder-length hair till the end of her trial, then had become a blonde except for her bangs, which were dyed pink, and she did the dye jobs and the haircuts on herself, giving herself a slightly ragged bob, thinking it made her look like nobody special.

While she was married to the late Kirk Biggins, she had learned how to get rid of one's old identity and assume a new one, so that was why she had been confident that it would be done for her thoroughly and effectively by the FBI and the US Marshals. They had transformed her into Jessica Baldwin. But by working in a boot and saddle store in a rodeo town in Montana, she had saved enough money to secretly obtain yet another set of credentials for herself and her child. . Katherine/Jessica had become Sarah and Magda had become Laura. Good riddance to the German name, Magdalena, that Kirk had put on her because it was the name of Joseph Goebbels's wife. Katherine had hated that name. She had learned that Joseph Goebbels's official title was Reich Minister for Enlightenment and Propaganda, the word "enlightenment" an oxymoron in Katherine's opinion though she didn't dare say so. When Hitler committed suicide in the Fuhrer Bunker, Joseph and Magda followed their Leader, first poisoning their six daughters and then themselves, obsequiously following Hitler to the end. Katherine had to inwardly scoff when she read that in his youth, Joseph Goebbels's favorite schoolteachers were Jewish, plus he was once engaged to a young woman who was part Jewish—but when it came to his own greed for power in the Nazi regime he was utterly ruthless.

By July of 20 Sarah and Laura Jamison were living in Philadelphia, a city big enough to get lost in, and a posthumous joke on the late Kirk, who had wanted to set off one of his dirty bombs there right after his massive hit on Boston where the Battle of Bunker Hill ignited the Revolution of 1776. Kirk's motive for utterly devastating the "City of Brotherly Love" was that it had hosted the Constitutional Convention of 1789 which had given birth to the American Republic.

Sarah hoped that no dirty bombs were going to explode in Boston or Philadelphia now that her husband was dead and his plans and devices had been confiscated—so far as the world knew. She wanted to believe that none of Kirk's former "confederates" were clever or intelligent enough to know how to build a crude nuclear device, but her insurance policy for herself and her daughter was a copy of an *Aryan Manifesto*—as Kirk had titled it—that she had stashed in a locker at a YWCA, its location never to be divulged to anyone unless she had to.

She feared an attack on herself or her daughter more than she feared a resumption of the bomb plot. She had absconded from Witness Protection mainly because she had come to distrust her handler. He had made thinly veiled advances toward her and had said one day, as if musing out loud, that if he chose to "put a bug in the wrong ears" he could make enough money to pay off his mortgage. He had quickly added, "Of course I would never do that." But she was appalled that a United States Marshal would toy with the idea of letting himself be corrupted. And she knew that if she dared to turn him in on such flimsy grounds it would be doubtful that anyone in a position of higher authority would believe her.

On top of her fears concerning her handler, she had found Witness Protection to be far from "warm and fuzzy." The government had provided her and her daughter with a plausible cover story and a monthly stipend that tided them over until they supposedly got acclimated. They also had gotten some sporadic counseling that was supposed to ease their adjustment into their new lives. But none of it was meant to last for a lifetime. Instead, in many ways they were stuck in a kind of limbo. They would never be able to go home again. Rebuilding their previous lives was not an option and not a concern of the Witness Protection Program. They had been made to "disappear" and if and when they should die, none of their friends or relatives would ever learn about it.

Sarah tried to adjust to her situation by telling herself over and over again that it made no difference if anybody or nobody knew what you had died of or where you were buried. The earth was a huge, unmarked grave for millions and millions of people down through the ages who would not be honored or even remembered. In any case, she couldn't think of anyone alive who truly would care about her and her daughter, even if they chose to resurface.

Except her grandfather, Roland Fornier, whom she had defied when she took up with Kirk Biggins. Yet hr grandfather hadn't disowned or given up on her. He had sat in the courtroom all through her trial. He had even nodded and flashed brief smiles at her, which she had dared to believe might be smiles of encouragement.

But she knew she would never see him again. Not only was she scared to confront him face to face, but if any diehard members of the Aryan Confederacy might be bent on tracking her down, they might try to get to her through her grandfather.

They might torture and kill him to get information they thought he might have—which he didn't have.

She had plenty of guilt on her shoulders that she would carry for the rest of her life, and she didn't want to absorb a shred more of it.

CHAPTER 4

At home in late evening after Vito decided to take on Roland's case, I was able to read up on the Aryan Confederacy thanks to Joy's research. My wife, Danielle, was on a girls' night out, so I was free to be by myself in my den with some hot tea with lemon and honey and a couple of raisin oatmeal cookies.

***

CONFIDENTAL MEMORANDUM
VICTOR MARTIN ASSOCIATES

THE ARYAN CONFEDERACY was founded by Conrad Pryzor, a rabid White supremacist and perpetrator of hate crimes that escalated to mass murder in the 1990s. He committed suicide in prison by slitting his wrists. His once powerful neo-Nazi organization, which had grown larger and larger over several decades, had maintained a large well-armed and heavily fortified compound in the outskirts of Washington, Pennsylvania, an area known as Klan Country North. They had their own radio station, their own courthouse to put defectors on trial, and even their own church wielding their own special "Holy Bible" full of passages extolling the superiority of the White race and the subjugation of all other races. They fancied themselves to be Aryan Knights Templars. They had their own Aryan Youth Brigade in which kids were taught obedience and discipline, endurance and teamwork, stoicism, and stealth. By the time they were made into full-fledged warriors they knew how to kill effectively in many ways, including how to employ a garrote or slit throats without making a sound. Conrad Pryzor was apparently inordinately proud of what he had wrought. But after his death, his followers splintered into small rival groups lusting to take over. There was a vicious power struggle and a weeding out, followed by a loose pulling together in hopes of a return to their "glory days."

Federal law enforcement agencies, including Homeland Security, have investigated a theory put forth by some defectors that the period of the most rapid growth of the Aryan Confederacy was due to the infiltration of their agents into the James Jones religious cult in Guyana. Hearsay has it that they were able to confiscate Jones's hoarded currency, jewelry, gold bars and silver bars after seven hundred of the cult's members, including Jones himself, killed themselves by drinking Kool Aid laced with cyanide. His treasure was rumored to be worth over a hundred million dollars.

Some of the worst of these terrorists are still on the loose. They are inspired by a novel entitled *The Turner Diaries* in which an army of super-patriots overthrows the United States government, massacres Jews and other non-Aryans, and annihilates Israel with nuclear weapons, thereby ushering in a Christian Paradise.

They assassinate judges and politicians because that sort of notoriety helps build their membership, but they also murder and rob because they dream of getting back to the kind of huge financial resources that they once enjoyed, which had enabled them to readily fund their anti-democratic missions.

Unfortunately the FBI, the ATF, and Homeland Security agents have been reduced to waiting for these mass murderers to make their moves before they can get onto them. Our law enforcement agencies try to anticipate where they will strike and be totally ready to take them out.

This leads me to suggest that if we are to find Roland Fortier's daughter we might have to resort to those same tactics. But of course, if that is to be our chosen route, we will have to employ it without bringing law enforcement down on *us*.

We will certainly need to discuss this further.

***

After reading all that, I was once again impressed by Joy's astuteness and thoroughness. I was proud of her. I thought she had hit the nail on the head.

But now the full implications, the perils, and the pain of what we were about to undertake, was overwhelming me. I was scared of what Roland was getting us into. And of what might ensue. I was sure none of us would back out. But what if he used us to help him get to the nutcases who were probably chasing Katherine and Magda, and had already decided that the White supremacists didn't deserve to live? I hated Nazis as much as he did. I was born in 1939, the year that Hitler invaded Poland, igniting World War Two, and before it was over, a hundred million people would be machine-gunned, burned to death, blown apart, or poisoned to death in gas chambers.

It was almost unbelievable to me that after all that human suffering and sacrifice we were allowing *neo*-Nazis to operate in the United States. What must the combat veterans of that war think about that anomaly? It made me want to weep when I thought about the veterans still living or long dead, who as young boys had stormed the Nazi machine-gun emplacements on the cliffs above the beaches in Normandy, knowing that they were going to take eighty percent casualties. They gave their all to defeat Nazism, only to come home and see it taking root in their own country.

What a kick in the balls that must be.

It made me think that I should almost stand back and applaud if Roland ended up gunning a couple of them down. Would my belief that nobody should take the law into his own hands hold up if push came to shove?

CHAPTER 5

Leroy Hubbard was the Pontifex Maximus of the mockery of a church that he had founded, and Jordan Giese was its Exalted Bishop. Those titles, conferred by Leroy himself, had a glorious history, and that's why Leroy had appropriated them. And he had named his church "The Church of the Creator," by which he meant the *Aryan Creator* and no other.

In ancient times, when Rome ruled the world, the Pontifex Maximus was the head of the Roman state religion and also the ruler of the Empire. Leroy believed that even though his domain was small right now, it would eventually out-perform Adolf Hitler's vision of the Thousand Year Reich. Hitler had also started out small, with a *Putsch* in a lowly beer hall that had landed him in a jail cell, from which he wrote his notorious autobiography, *Mein Kamp*, i.e., *My Struggle*.

On a beautiful summer day Leroy Hubbard and Jordan Giese were in the front seat of a white Ford Bronco on their way to the home of Judge Ruth Steingart, a "stinking Jew" who had ruled against Leroy in a copyright infringement suit, decreeing that he had no legal right to the title "Church of the Creator" because a Christian congregation had registered that name some years prior with the United States Copyright Office. Leroy Hubbard was outraged that a Jewish judge would knuckle under to a bunch of immersion-baptism Holy Rollers. The goddamn bitch! She had ruled in the Christian lawyer's favor on every motion that he had put before her. Therefore, she had to die.

Leroy Hubbard, later anointed by himself as a Pontifex Maximus, was born in Lansing, Michigan, in 1971. Under the virtually absent "guidance" of his father, a policeman who never managed to rise in the ranks, Leroy became a viciously angry and willful child, then a viciously angry pre-teen who decided he was a White supremacist before he reached puberty. During his twenties and thirties, he committed property crimes and attacks on gays and lesbians, beating them so viciously that his reputation for unmitigated and unremorseful violence made him a contender for leadership among other neo-Nazis. When Abel Brunswick, the founder of the Church of the Creator, died in state prison of multiple shank wounds delivered to him by a Black fellow prisoner, Leroy declared himself Brunswick's successor.

One of Hubbard's first acts as the new Pontifex Maximus was to sign a pact with Conrad Pryzor's Aryan Confederacy. This was a tactful move that consolidated their power. But the truth was that he privately considered Pryzor to be a weak leader and prided himself knowing he was much more aggressive.

Under Hubbard, the Manifesto of the Church of the Creator mandated that "The flames of anti-Semitism will soon be fanned into an all-consuming rage of extinction. The Jews are evil incarnate. The White Race must cease to subsidize the mud races. Instead we need to enslave them, outright eliminate them, or punish them through neglect to make them wither on the vine.

"The White race has created and funded all of the world's progress. Our legacy of accomplishments towers above the ignorant whining, groveling, and meager contributions of the mud races. They impede progress and must be exterminated for the good of mankind.

"The Judeo-Christian God is a shallow invention of superstitious and uneducated ancient Hebrew tribes. Our Aryan God is all-powerful and will have no other gods before Him, and we are conceived in His Image. We will wage a righteous Holy War that will establish our just rule over Christianity and Judaism."

In his early days, in spite of these vociferous rants in mailings and on the Web, Leroy Hubbard had almost no dues-paying followers. His mother was long gone, and he didn't know where, and his father might as well have not been in his life for all the parenting that he did. What Hubbard unabashedly called his "world headquarters" was his own bedroom in his father's house in a shabby rundown section of Lansing. He used an Israeli flag as a doormat for wiping his muddy boots and painted the walls red to symbolize blood that had been heroically shed by White warriors. But he kept teddy bears on the pillows of his bed, as if he had not matured out of his early stage as a sad and angry child.

In high school, his classmates considered him awkward and stilted, and he had almost no friends and little desire to make any. After graduation he studied political science at Michigan State but hardly ever attended class and did not stay past his junior year. In a farewell note to his landlord in an envelope containing a check for only half of what he owed, he stated that he was "embarking on a mission that was destined to be his life's work."

He didn't have any criminal record at this time. But one of his skinhead pals, Lance Hargood, went on a shooting spree in a shopping center, killing two Hispanics and wounding three African Americans, then shot himself in the head as police closed in on him. Although Leroy Hubbard was investigated and grilled heavily as a suspected instigator of Hargood's rampage, the evidence against him was too weak, and he was not charged. In the aftermath, he laid low but continued to use direct mail to collect dues and recruit more members for his Church of the Creator. The FBI estimated that by the 1990s he had about three hundred dues-paying members even though he was claiming over 80,000. However, the publicity from Hargood's killing spree caused membership to mushroom, possibly to as many as 2,600.

Then came the lawsuit by the owners of a rival entity also calling itself the Church of the Creator. It was an off-the-wall Christian congregation that had only one house of worship—and for a while Leroy Hubbard and Jordan Giese considered the quick and easy expedient of bombing it to smithereens. But since they were its target in the lawsuit right now, they would quickly be suspected and probably arrested and convicted. So they had to go to court. Predictably, the biased Jewish judge had ruled against them.

She had made her own bed and now she had to lie in it. The Pontifex Maximus had declared her "an enemy of the Aryan people" and had sentenced her to die.

CHAPTER 6

Judge Ruth Steingart was under no illusion that irrational hatred of those who were "different" would ever cease being a trait of what Mark Twain had called *The Damned Human Race*. In an essay of that title, he satirized our vainglorious notions of ourselves and our rank in the universe, concluding that humans aren't the highest animal but the lowest. With his usual acerbic wit and brilliant prose, he "proved" that the difference between an earl and an anaconda was that the earl would wantonly slaughter other animals for sport, whereas an anaconda would kill one animal at a time and only when he was hungry. His intent was to show that the buffalo hunters of his time, far from being heroes, were killing off the buffalo herds to starve the Native Americans into extinction.

Even as a young girl, Ruth was deeply concerned about social, political and cultural matters, and as she grew wiser, she was acutely aware that nothing had changed. Man's cruelty toward man was always on full display. Her European grandparents had died in gas chambers.

For over two thousand years Pogroms against Jews had been a staple of European rulers and angry mobs. Anti-Semitism was still alive in most countries of the world, and in the United States it was very much on the rise.

Nevertheless, Ruth was an optimist. Or tried to be. She wanted to make a positive difference while she was here on earth. She was not a practicing Jew in the literal sense, but she had reverence for her roots and the beliefs of her ancestors. She was proud of her heritage. And as an idealistic teenager she wanted to find her true calling.

After graduating from high school, she majored in American literature at Drake University and took enough courses in secondary education to go into teaching. But the disciplinary problems she knew she would face led her to enroll in law school. She was passionate about civil rights, women's rights, voting rights, and other social issues, so she thought she might apply for a position with the American Civil Liberties Union. But while she was studying for her bar exam her husband walked out on her, leaving her to raise their two-year-old son all alone. She was so furious over the desertion and her ensuing battle for child support that she joined a firm specializing in family law so she could sharpen her sense of what to do in her own situation. Then, after three years in the trenches, she accepted a position with a firm of criminal defense lawyers where she hoped to be an advocate for people wrongly accused, but instead she found that in order to be an effective defender she often had to fool herself into a belief in the innocence of people who were most likely guilty. This was too gut-wrenching for her, and so when she was offered a job as an assistant district attorney, she accepted it. A decade later she was elected to a judgeship, and her jurisdiction was in Harrisburg, the capital city of Pennsylvania. Most of the obstacles she presided over were rather mundane, but some were more intriguing, and some were full of vitriol and resulted in death threats. But her firm belief in the rule of law was not to be deterred.

She believed that Leroy Hubbard, the self-proclaimed "Pontifex Maximus" of the Church of the Creator, was indeed a very dangerous man. The lexicon of evil deeds that he was *thought* to have committed, greatly exceeded the relative few that he had been convicted and punished for. Like Conrad Pryzor, who had died in infamy, Leroy Hubbard was wily enough to insulate himself from the cronies and henchmen who followed his orders. They went to jail out of rabid loyalty to him, while he went unpunished.

Judge Ruth Steingart was afraid Hubbard's minions might be coming for her sooner rather than later. Right in front of her he had screamed out his vow of revenge, proclaiming that he was "the fiery sword of the God of Aryans."

She would not be surprised if, now that he had lost in court, he would start calling his church The Church of the *Fiery* Aryan God. But a much better name for it would be the Church of Unbridled Hatred.

CHAPTER 7

The Pontifex Maximus and his Exalted Bishop cruised past the judge's house in their white Ford Bronco on a bright summer day in early June. Leroy Hubbard was in the passenger seat and Jordan Giese was driving at a careful fifteen miles per hour so he wouldn't alarm anyone who might catch a peek at them. They wanted a quick drive-by look at the judge's place in case somebody had shown up to trim the lawn or cut the hedges and might interfere with their plans. They wanted to be able to make a quick entry and a clean exit after the kill.

It was over six months now since the judge heard their case and ruled against them. In that period of watchful dormancy, they bided their time until the tight security around her had been eased, which is what they had been counting on. A couple days ago, they chortled when they saw her on TV trying to appear courageous but sounding rattled. There was a catch in her throat, almost a stutter, when she said, "I've handed stiff sentences to many a convicted felon, and I refuse to be afraid of them."

"Well, well, well, we'll see about *that*, you Jew *bitch!*" Leroy shouted at the TV, and he and Jordan jumped up and high-fived each other. They thought that Judge Steingart had just confirmed their belief that stubbornness and pride would cause her to seek a too hasty return to normality, and she would shed her protectors. They had little doubt that by now she must be more vulnerable than she once was. But just to be sure, over the past several weeks Pontifex Maximus had dispatched several of his underlings in various kinds of vehicles and in different disguises, with orders to scout the target and make sure she was no longer closely guarded. All of their reports were satisfactory. Now the issue was, how were they going to get at her? She lived in an upscale community that was an ideal place for families to raise their children because it was so peaceful and quiet and bereft of crime. They considered a blitz attack—just sneak into the backyard with a battering ram like the ones cops use when they're making an unannounced arrest, bash in the kitchen door with a couple of hard blows, then charge in with the advantage of surprise and take the judge out with a barrage of shots from their 9mm Glocks.

They had the heavy iron battering ram in the cargo bay of their black Bronco. But luck was with them, and they found that they wouldn't have to actually use it. They perked up because on their second slow drive past Judge Steingart's ritzy residence, they saw the garage door go up to let her back out. She was driving a late-model silver BMW—but unfortunately, she wasn't alone. There was someone in the passenger seat.

"Dig the dude that's with her," said Jordon Giese, a note of alarm in his voice. "You wanna back off?"

Leroy Hubbard immediately said, "Uh-uh. I don't think we have to. All indications have been that the cops aren't around anymore. He's probably just a friend or a relative."

"I should just follow her?"

"Absolutely. We'll pick a good place to pull alongside them and pump a full clip at them. They won't know what hit 'em."

Jordan gloated. "I'll be the shooter, then. You'll be on the opposite side of them and your hands will have to be on the wheel."

"Piece of cake," Leroy said. "For a couple of bad shots."

They laughed in self-mockery because neither one of them was an expert marksman. They could admit it and take it in stride because they were leaders, not peons. They didn't practice every other week on a shooting range and they didn't toss bottles in the air and shatter them with bullets like Butch Cassidy and the

Sundance Kid. Up close and personal was their motif. Soft hot lead to the base of the skull, the forehead, or the chest, close enough to leave powder burns while blowing big holes through bones and organs. Jordan couldn't miss if he was right alongside Judge Steingart's vehicle, just a couple feet away from her face and head.

But they had no idea where she was headed today in her spiffy BMW, and they didn't want to do her in a crush of traffic or a jam at a traffic light, where they wouldn't be able to speed away ahead of any wailing sirens. They had to wait for an opportune situation for pumping their bullets into her, then stomping on the gas for their quick and clean getaway.

"I hope she's heading for a mall," Leroy said.

And Jordan said, *"Ha!* You called it, *didn't* you?" because she took a turnoff for the Quaker Run Mall, not very far from her residential neighborhood.

As they followed her at a discrete distance so they wouldn't alarm her or her passenger, Jordan said, "The fuckin' kikes are stupid. Neither one is using their mirrors to make sure they aren't being followed. They're not even turnin' their heads."

Leroy said. "I hope she parks in a slot without any other vehicles too close to her."

He grinned when, just as he had wished, Judge Steingart pulled into a slot with another empty slot to her left.

"Yes!" Jordan blurted triumphantly. His eyes flicked left and right, casing the lot for nosy onlookers, and not spotting any, as he pulled into the slot that was the perfect place for an ambush.

"Do it quick so we can split!" Leroy commanded. "Get your damn gun out." Then he pushed the button that let the passenger-side window slide down.

But Jordan was already getting out of the Bronco, only a foot or so from Judge Steingart, pointing his Glock at her. Her window was up, but it wasn't likely to be bulletproof glass, so he knew his bullets would shatter it to pieces.

He started to tighten his finger on his trigger.

But just then Judge Steingart's passenger—a big square-jawed guy with a buzz-cut—jumped out and aimed a big, looming, chrome-plated revolver at Jordan right over the top of the BMW.

Blam! Jordan fired at the judge's head and shattered glass flew at him, so he ducked.

Then the buzz-cut guy fired at *him!* Jordan's head exploded, gushing blood, and the shocked look on his face slackened and faded as he dropped his Glock and went down.

Leroy was totally panicked, ducking his head as low as he could, almost onto the steering column. Then he peeled out, side-swiping the judge's BMW, his tires squealing, burning rubber on the asphalt. A bullet missed his head by inches. It shattered his windshield—and four quick follow-up shots punched holes in the Bronco.

"Fuck!" Leroy yelled, scared his gas tank would explode.

He almost couldn't believe he made it onto the highway.

He heard sirens wailing and was pretty sure he would be caught.

He wondered if he would have the guts to martyr himself before he was captured or killed. Images of two of his most fervent idols, Nazi Reichsmarshalls Heinrich Himmler and Herman Goering, flashed through his mind. When he was about twelve years old, he had seen postmortem photos of them in a mildewed World War Two magazine that his father had kept on a shelf in the basement. The captions said that they had both swallowed cyanide capsules in order to deprive their enemies of hanging them. They were lying flat on their backs, their faces grotesquely distorted in their final agony. The accompanying article had pointed out that dying by cyanide poisoning was excruciatingly painful.

Leroy drove faster, sometimes as much as twenty miles per hour over the speed limit, as the desperation to escape overwhelmed him.

CHAPTER 8

Joy said, "According to the *Philadelphia Enquirer*, Judge Steingart started to feel a little too safe after about six months had gone by since the copyright infringement trial against Leroy Hubbard. She thought police protection could be called off because she had her son Avrom to take it over. He had just gone through a divorce, so he moved in with her—and he's a CIA officer. The judge raised him from age two on up after her husband abandoned both of them. Avrom must be a helluva guy. This wasn't his first shootout, wasn't even his most lethal."

The attempt on the judge's life had happened two days ago, all the way on the other side of Pennsylvania. Philadelphia was almost three hundred miles from Pittsburgh, but we were alert for anything that appeared to involve neo-Nazis.

Vito said, "Judge Steingart was just doing her job in a simple civil case, but Hubbard couldn't stand it. She didn't make it out of the ICU. The bullet caused her brain to swell and her son had to make the decision to take her off of life support. Too bad he couldn't have killed both of those assholes."

I said, "Luckily, they turned out to be a pair of inept clowns. But even inept people can be extremely dangerous these days."

"I know what you mean," Joy said sadly. "I can't believe the crazy stuff that goes down in this country anymore. It's because we have more guns than people—armed with heavy firepower that soldiers used to carry, not civilians. It didn't used to be that way, so the founding fathers didn't take it into account. Try pulling off a mass shooting if you're armed with a single-shot musket that takes three minutes to load."

"You'd maybe kill just one person," Vito said, "before you got beaten to death with your own musket."

I said, "You can record a hit song with your own garage band or, if you're Kirk Biggins, you can use it as a place to build fissionable bombs."

"You can even make a truck bomb filled with combustible fertilizer like Timothy McVeigh did," Joy said. "Talk about a *shit* storm!"

Vito flashed her a sardonic smirk.

Joy said to me, "Dad? Did Roland's granddaughter really say right in court that she had committed a *hate* crime?"

"She did according to Roland. She said she was a victim of violent abuse from Kirk Biggins, and she built up enough hate to stand over him and pull the trigger."

"I *like* her for doing it. I can't help it," Joy said.

"Score one for the good guys," Vito agreed. "A hate crime in reverse. What goes around comes around. Trouble is, the rule of law goes out the window."

"Well, it saved Boston and who knows how many other cities," I said. "God only knows how many churches and synagogues."

Vito said, "But these nutcases are not about to stop. So let's start figuring out what *we're* gonna do. There are way too many neo-Nazis in this country besides the Aryan Confederacy or what's left of it, and we don't know which particular outfit or splinter group Biggins was hooked up with besides his own thing, that church of something or other."

"Church of the Creator," I said. "More like Church of the Destroyer."

"I didn't sleep very much last night," Joy said. "I had to put on makeup this morning to hide the puffy bags under my eyes. While I was filling myself up with black coffee, I thought maybe we should get in touch with the ACLU or the Southern Poverty Law Center because they monitor all the domestic terrorist groups that come to their attention. They might even have a dossier on Biggins. I bet they started building one on him and his asshole buddies after Katherine killed him and his bomb plot was revealed."

"Good thinking," Vito said. "Don't get me wrong, I want to help Roland. But I also want to stop some other gang of assholes from setting off a dirty bomb of their own."

CHAPTER 9

A scowling shaky-looking gunman suddenly appeared in Hayley Hunter's backyard coming through the gate of the redwood fence while she was sunning herself on the deck of the above-ground pool. She saw his gun before she saw *him*—but she stifled her scream in hopes that he wouldn't shoot her if she didn't yell for help.

She was pretty sure who he was because *Breaking News* had interrupted the retro disco music she was listening to on her mother's old-fashioned boom box. It was part of the score from *Grease*, starring John Travolta and Olivia Newton-John. Hayley had been singing along, adding her own voice to some of the songs, because she was going to be one of the singers in her senior class play, a vignette of scenes from that Oscar-winning musical of the 1970s.

Hayley was seventeen years old, a high school cheerleader, a sprinter on the track team, a valedictorian. On the Honor Roll ad destined for college. But now she was scared that if she made a wrong move or if the man with the gun got antsy, none of her dreams would come true. Maybe she should have screamed to alert her parents. But that might've turned out badly. The gunman probably would have shot her right away, then chased her mother and father down and killed *them*.

"Don't you dare gimme any trouble, sweetheart," he snarled at her. "I just need keys to one of your family cars. I might have to tie you up, but I won't kill you. Not if you cooperate. Anybody else in the house?"

"Just my parents. Please don't hurt us."

"You lead and I'll be right behind you so they won't try anything. I don't think they will when they see my gun jabbing into you."

Hayley knew that there was no way that either her mom or her dad could go up against this man even if she screamed out a warning. They didn't keep guns in the house. They didn't even own any. It was a matter of principle with them. They were contributors to the PAC that was set up to advocate for the Brady Bill, which was named after an aide to President Ronald Reagan who was shot in the head during an attempt by a lone wolf to assassinate the president. Hayley didn't see that she had a choice. She had to lead the gunman into her home and right toward her parents. She only hoped that one of them wouldn't panic and bolt and get shot.

As she crept into the house through the back door and into the kitchen with the man's gun prodding her, she had no way of knowing that a police squad was already in the alley outside of the redwood fence. They had parked their vehicles a block away and had crept in on foot. In the immediate aftermath of the attempt on Judge Steingart's life, they had gotten the Bronco's license plate number from a sharp-eyed lady with a bag of groceries, which enabled them to put out a BOLO. The Be On the Lookout alert had led to the spotting of the Bronco parked in the alley. On their way there, the cops had called in a SWAT team and a hostage negotiator.

Inside the house, unaware of all this, Leroy Hubbard forced Hayley's dad to lie on the living room floor while her mom tied his wrists and ankles, using a cord from an electric toaster and another cord from a lamp. Then he ordered Hayley to use a couple of cords from other appliances to tie up her mom.

Lastly, he tied Hayley's hands behind her back with a computer cord, and when he was finished he said, "You're gonna get a free ride. I'm takin' you with me."

At that moment, the hostage negotiator's voice boomed from his megaphone.

"This is the police. You are surrounded. Come out with your hands up. Hostages must come out first. Then the hostage taker. If you defy this order, you do it at your peril."

The announcement was greeted by a long, suspenseful moment of silence.

From inside the house, Leroy Hubbard peeled back a gauzy curtain and squinted through a kitchen window above the sink. Nobody was in the yard. But to him it was a certainty that men in assault helmets and protective garments, heavily armed with assault weapons were in tactical positions surrounding the house from cover.

The old, mildewed photos of the two dead Reichsmarshalls flashed through his mind, and he began to sweat profusely.

Again, the voice of the hostage negotiator boomed out.

"I repeat that you are surrounded. Come out with your hands up. Do not defy this order or you will be killed."

Once again there was a long moment of silence.

Then a single gunshot.

The back door of the house slowly came open.

Then Hayley stepped out shaking and crying for fear of getting shot due to the fact her wrists were tied and she couldn't put her hands up.

She looked at the hostage negotiator, his face barely peeking out at her as he crouched behind the corner of the above-ground swimming pool.

Her mouth was so dry she could barely get the words out, but she said, "Please don't shoot me! He's dead! He killed himself, thank God!"

CHAPTER 10

Our investigative team, headed by Vito, and backed up by Joy, with me as an adjunct member, met with Roland Fornier so we could all get acquainted in person. As it turned out, Vito knew Roland from back when he was "that jailbird's son" and had arrested him a couple of times for DUIs or fistfights.

"You were a terror as a teenager," Vito told him as they shook hands.

They both laughed and clapped each other on the shoulder. Roland was wearing a gray plaid suit with an open-necked white silk shirt and no vest or tie. Vito and I were dressed casually, as usual, in jeans and short-sleeved shirts, and Joy was wearing a blue skirt and a light-blue blouse and no makeup. She looked alert and primed for business, so I assumed she had gotten more sleep last night than she had the day before.

We were ushered to our table by a balding middle-aged waiter in a limp red bowtie and a white waistcoat with sleeves frayed at the cuffs.

"Your daughter's beautiful," Roland turned toward me and said.

Joy liked to be talked to, not about, but she let it slide.

I was surprised when Roland wanted to meet at The King's Castle, a seedy rundown nightclub on Route 51, only a few miles from Clairton. If you drove north for twelve miles on 51 it took you into Pittsburgh through the Liberty Tunnels, and if you drove south for thirty miles you'd reach the small rural city of Uniontown, not far from Fort Necessity, a small, reconstructed log blockhouse and stockade that I had loved to visit as a child anytime my parents would take me there. The original was built by George Washington's Colonial militia men at the outset of the French and Indian War when they were greatly outnumbered by enemy troops in hot pursuit. Washington lost the skirmish and had to surrender his sword, but he learned valuable lessons that enabled him to defeat the British in the American Revolution and become honored as the Father of His Country.

Many of my horror fans would be stunned if they found out I'm a history buff, but I firmly believe we need to know where we came from so we know where we're going or have any hope of figuring out where we *should* be going. One of the characters in my book, *Dealey Plaza,* says, "A country that doesn't know its own history is like a man with amnesia." Over the past few days, prospects of dirty bombs and neo-Nazi terrorists had me in a state of heightened awareness about our precious heritage and perilous future.

Vito and Joy and I wanted to update Roland on the things we had learned so far and pump him for whatever else he might know that could help us implement some kind of strategy, even if it had to be loosely constructed for the time being. When we were seated at our table, Roland said, "I wanted to come here to see Jocko's murals again."

"I sort of figured that," I told him.

The walls of The King's Castle were covered with chipped and fading paintings of knights being knighted and princesses being courted and jolly peasants roasting a pig on a spit. In the 1970s the owner had paid an artist named Jack "Jocko" Randolph, one of Roland Fornier's best buddies, to paint those scenes on the walls. Back then, before they were chipped and faded, most of the diners greatly admired the murals, but I always thought they looked like scenes and characters from Walt Disney's animated films like *Cinderella* or *Sleeping Beauty.*

However, I always got a big kick out of Jack Randolph. At six feet tall and three hundred and thirty-some pounds, he was a ferociously loud and rambunctious biker, brawler, weightlifter, and self-taught artist who wore a black tam while he kicked people's asses. I had often worked out with him in his backyard or browsed through jazz albums in the record store he once owned, so I had fond memories of him, just like Roland did. He was yet another person that I hadn't seen in a long time.

The food in The King's Castle used to be decent, but now it wasn't. We were all eating spaghetti and meatballs—which reminded me of how much Roland loved my mom's pasta back when we were teenagers, except the stuff in front of us today was more like Chef Boyardee.Roland said, "This ain't like your mother's," and we all laughed.

I wryly hoped that trying to come up with a plan for our ensuing investigation might take our minds off of the bad food. I almost said it out loud. We couldn't afford to dilly-dally. Not only did we need to find Katherine ande Magda, we had to put a stop to anybody who still wanted to build a dirty bomb.

As soon as we were finished eating and were served coffee, Joy opened the embossed leather briefcase I had bought her for Christmas and handed Roland copies of her research printouts Vito and I already had.

"I should've emailed these to you to save time," she said.

Roland said, "No matter. I'm a speed reader."

I didn't know that about him, but it seemed to be true. When he laid the reports aside, Vito allowed Joy to take the lead. "Did any of the names you just saw jog your memory in any way?" she asked him.

He thought about it but shook his head no.

"You're sure you haven't heard of them before now?" she persisted. "Primarily Leroy Hubbard or Jordan Giese."

"Nope," Roland answered. "I had very little contact with Katherine after she married Kirk Biggins. The main thing that stuck out was that he belonged to something called the Aryan Confederacy, as if they wanted to launch another White people's

48

war against the government like the South did during the Civil War."

"Yeah. You hit the nail on the head," Vito acknowledged. "Their aim is to overthrow our democracy and turn this country into a Christian theocracy for White people only. No others need apply."

On that note we were impelled to start laying out our makeshift ideas, such as getting in touch either with the ACLU or the Southern Poverty Law Center. For the time being, we didn't come up with much more than that, so we figured it would at least be a start that we could build on and maybe take it in a more focused direction depending on whatever we learned.

Roland said, "Well, look, I'm basically up shit creek without a paddle. I don't know any more than what I already told you. I'm depending on you and Joy, Vito. And even my old pal here." He reached out and clapped me on the shoulder. "So what's this gonna cost me?"

Vito said, "My standard rate is five-hundred dollars an hour. But only for the hours when I'm actually doing something. And it covers Joy, too. She's on salary."

"Well, I don't expect any kind of special deal. I'm capable of paying whatever you say. Let me show you something."

Roland reached into the inside pocket of his suit jacket, pulled out a folded magazine article and straightened it and laid it in the center of the table so we could all look at it. It had a gaudy red headline: "The Man Who Found a Spanish Galleon!" And there he was in the lead photo, tanned golden and in bathing trunks, looking as fit and trim as a much younger and very athletic man.

"That can't be you," I joked with him.

He said, "This is what I've been into in Florida, where I've been living for the past nine years. I made a lot of money selling gambling machines to the Native American casinos, and I invested a pile of it into this outfit that searches for shipwrecks under the ocean. Last year we found one and pulled it up and salvaged three million dollars in fifteenth-century treasure in oaken chests broken open by the passage of time, spilling out jewels and gold and silver."

"Only you!" I said with an unsuppressed laugh.

"Amazing!" said Vito.

"Wow!" Joy gasped.

Vito and I, both being Clairtonites born and bred, were well aware of Roland's exploits as a youngster, some triumphant and others reminiscent of Don Qixote tilting at a windmill. In our junior year in high school a huge riot broke out over a disputed call at a junior varsity football game and five guys there rooting for the opposing team grabbed Roland and shoved him over the top of the bleachers. It was about a thirty-foot fall and he landed on hard ground, but he ran back to the top of the bleachers, and in the midst of the brawl he threw off each of the guys who had thrown him off—only to find out later that he did it with a broken arm.

I asked him to tell that story for Vito and Joy, but he didn't want to. In fact, he seemed a little embarrassed by it.

Just then our middle-aged waiter brought a big stranger to our table—at least I thought it was a stranger—but Roland jumped up laughing and threw his arms around him and then I realized who it was—and by god, it was Jocko Randolph! I hadn't known if he was alive or dead, but there he was in the flesh—and not so much of it as in years past. He must've lost about fifty or sixty pounds, yet he was still bigger around than Roland was, but he looked suave and quite dapper, resplendently dressed in a black pinstriped suit with a light-blue shirt and a gaudy necktie.

"You don't know who I am, *do* you, Mr. Filmmaker!" he bellowed at me.

I said, "Sure I do, Jocko." He hugged me so hard I thought my chest was being crushed.

"Sit down, sit down, Jocko," Roland said, pulling a chair over from a neighboring table. Then he said, "Jocko and I partnered up to sell the gambling machines to the casinos, then we both invested in the salvage outfit that spent years searching for that Spanish galleon and finally found it. After that, a team of expert divers did the really dangerous stuff, using massive woven rope nets and bringing the treasure up a little at a time with a crane. Lucky none of them got killed doing it. The bends, you know, and there were also sharks."

My only knowledge of all that was what I had seen in a couple of movies when I was a kid, but I could vaguely picture it. Joy seemed impressed, but Vito remained blasé.

We decided we should have a round or two of drinks, so we ordered a fifth of bourbon with cracked ice in a bucket, and after we got a bit liquored up, Roland started telling the story about the time Jocko wrestled an orangutan. It sounds preposterous, but it's true. I was sitting in the stands with Roland at the dinky little carnival where it happened, and it became one of my favorite stories to tell fellow pot-smokers back in my college days when I used to regularly get stoned.

As Roland, Jocko, and I drove to the carnival, at the bottom part of Clairton where the coke works was, we were in our early twenties and none of us had much money. We wanted to at least be able to buy some quarts of beet—Carling's Black Label was thirty-five cents a quart back then—and Jocko said, "I heard this carnival has a gimmick going where you can box a chimpanzee or wrestle an orangutan, and if you can stay in the ring for ten minutes you win a hundred bucks."

"Damn! I wouldn't mind a hundred smackers," Roland said. "Let's team up and do it."

"Well, I hate to tell you this," said Jocko, "but I heard that the chimpanzee damn near ripped some guy's balls off and they needed to be surgically reattached."

"So why don't we do the orangutan," Roland promptly suggested. "You want in on this, Dave?"

"Hell, no!" I said. "I'm gonna need my balls for a while."

"If you ever get laid!" Jocko said, snickering at me.

Roland said. "We'll still buy you some beer when we win."

"So let's draw straws," Jocko said. "No way can a fuckin' dumb animal beat two of us in a row. Whoever draws the short straw will go in the cage first and soften the beast up. Then the other one will come in for the kill."

"What're you gonna do, strangle him?" I asked him.

"No, you just gotta stay in for ten minutes. Piece of cake."

He puffed out his enormous chest, beaming proudly at the fact he and Roland were both wearing black skin-tight Muscleman T-shirts they had ordered by mail from a body-building magazine.

When we parked the car in a crowded lot and got out, Roland picked up some twigs and broke them into short pieces and handed them to me so he and Jocko could each draw one and compare them to each other. Jocko lost, so he had to go in the cage first and we laughed at him and mocked him and wished him good luck.

"Bring home the bacon!" Roland said as he and I headed for the stands and Jocko headed toward the cage, where the barker did his spiel, asked him if he was sure he wanted to risk his life, then got him to put on a thick leather belt that was wide enough in front to protect his balls, plus a helmet with a chin strip that was like the cheap leatherette football helmet my mom bought me at the five-and-dime when I was nine years old. Then the barker opened the cage door and pushed the orangutan to the back of the cage, using a ten-foot-long pole.

Jocko strode into the cage and the barker shut the door—and immediately the orangutan started shrieking and leaping and bouncing from one side of the cage to the next—till it crashed into Jocko's chest.

In half a second there was nothing left of Jocko's black T-shirt but part of a sleeve and the ring around the neck.

Jocko got the orangutan in a bear hug and was trying to crush it into submission like he had done to many a guy in a bar fight, but the orangutan grabbed Jocko's helmet and ripped it to pieces while with one of its feet it started pulling the leather belt to one side and with its other knee it started hammering Jocko's solar plexus like a ball peen hammer at high speed. It looked like Jocko was doomed. He would either get his balls ripped off or his head kicked in.

But the orangutan let loose of him and started leaping from one side of the cage to next, just like before.

That's when the barker came to the rescue with his ten-foot-pole and prodded the animal to the back of the cage again.

He said to Jocko, "You still wanna stay in?" "Fuck no!" Jocko said. "Lemme outta here!"

So the barker gave him three dollars because he had stayed in the cage for three minutes, plus a certificate making him a member of the Royal Society of Ape Fighters.

All the people in the stands were yelling, whistling, and applauding when he came up to where Roland I were, and we saw how bruised his face and chest were, but he said to Roland, "The thing is softened up. Your turn to volunteer. We gotta get that hundred bucks."

"Well, I'm sorry but I'm gonna welch," Roland said. "No way am I goin' in there."

We all laughed, and Jocko didn't get mad because that wouldn't be considered cool. We thought it was great that we now had another good story to tell.

Joy listened as we rehashed it, looking not entirely sure of when she should laugh or when she should just clam up and listen. "All you guys are too much!" she finally said.

Roland said, "Jocko and I have got people to see and things to do. So we're gonna take off. It's a deal about the five-hundred

53

an hour. Stay in touch as soon as you guys learn anything or make contact with anybody helpful."

Vito promised we would, and he and Joy and I stayed a while longer to share our impressions of what went down.

"I'm anxious to keep going on this," Joy said.

"So am I," said Vito. "What are your thoughts, Dave?"

"I'd love to put the bomb makers out of business. But at the same time, I think Roland and Jocko might go rogue."

"It's a possibility," Vito agreed. "We'll have to be careful how we play anything we discover. We've got to clue Roland in at all times, but we can't let him and Jocko upstage us—I mean go in under a black flag, so to speak."

I looked at Joy, and when her eyes met mine I said, "I'm probably thinking the same thing you are, honey. If anybody gets killed it better be the right people. And our hands have to stay clean. Helping Roland doesn't mean we want our lives to be ruined."

CHAPTER 11

The truth was that Sarah had not liked working in the boot and saddle store and had resisted getting acclimated to the scorching summer sun or bitter winter blizzards in Montana. She preferred the temperate climate and cosmopolitan demeanor in Philadelphia. And nowadays she was making a good living doing people's taxes. Her employer was a small company that operated pretty much like H&R Block but had only three branch offices instead of hundreds. Gilmore Associates LLC was privately owned, not traded publicly, and not on the stock exchange, which suited Sarah just fine because she didn't want to work for any entity that had high visibility.

Ironically, she owed her accounting expertise to her vicious, brutal husband. He had allowed her to enroll in a community college and go for a paralegal certificate, not out of love and affection for her, but for the benefit of the Aryan Confederacy. His pipedream was that he would revive the Confederacy and recruit thousands of new followers once he became its glorious Leader. He thought that such a huge organization would need to utilize the expertise of all types of hirelings and volunteers including lawyers and accountants, and his wife would be one of them, under his thumb and taking her marching orders from him. He believed that he could achieve all this once he became one of the greatest heroes the Aryan Race had ever known by detonating his fissionable bombs and sparking a full-fledged fascist revolution. In between threats and beatings, Sarah had heard his rants and his diatribes many times over when he was drunk or drugged up. She thought he would always be nothing but a thug and a peon who liked to blow things up. His vision of a New World Order was poppycock. He would never become a leader of anything except his own distorted ego.

Sarah remained ever wary and yet thankful that she and Laura, who was six years old now, were living in a modest apartment in South Philly, a part of the city that abounded in delicious Chinese and Italian food. They had their choice of fabulous cuisine, either eat-in or takeout. Every time they ate pasta with meatballs, it made Sarah think of her grandfather because it was his favorite. He had told her of his pal back in his high school days whose mother cooked the best Italian food ever. He said that this pal had become a famous movie director, and his name was David Cristi. Back when her name was Katherine, Sarah had seen *Intensive Scare Part Three*. She was proud to know that the director had actually grown up in Clairton, Pennsylvania, originally where her grandfather, Roland Fornier, was from.

After quite a few years of pushing him out of her mind, she no longer thought very much about her grandfather, and when she did, she didn't think that she missed him. But she did believe that her little girl needed a male figure in her life, and one who was an antidote to the creep she had blindly married.

Like many immature teenagers, she had bucked against the adults in her life—people who sincerely wanted to guide her and protect her—including teachers, guidance counselors, and her own grandfather. Even back then a part of her had realized that he was doing things for her own good, or at least he thought he was, but she was too rebellious to obey him. Especially when she believed she was in love. But now she had recognized her own naiveté. Now that it had become too late. Or was it?

Sometimes she couldn't help wondering what it would have been like if she made contact with her grandfather again.

Would he cry and give her a big welcoming hug?

Or would he tell her to go away and never come back?

CHAPTER 12

Jastin and Sajan Eckert were riding in Jastin's black Blazer and Jastin was driving. They were headed toward the defunct Aryan Confederacy compound, wiped out by the Pennsylvania State Troopers and FBI SWAT teams just a few years ago. Harboring a deep nostalgia for their glory days, they wanted to roam through their hallowed grounds about how grand it all used to be. They felt lucky to be able to come back here. After all, neither Heinrich Himmler nor Adolf Mengele nor the commandant of Auschwitz ever got to revisit their old haunts.

The two brothers both used to be lieutenants in the highly trained and well-armed Aryan Confederacy militia. Because they were off on a search and kill mission against some Jewish agitators in Michigan, along with their squad captain, Kirk Biggins, they had not been maimed or killed, like so many of their comrades, when government forces stormed the compound. In the aftermath, deprived of the huge, menacing presence that the Aryan Confederacy once used to be, they had become renegades, thirsting for revenge, and working with Kirk Biggins and his goal of planting homemade nuclear devices in Boston and Philadelphia and then elsewhere.

Now Kirk was dead, shot by his treacherous wife, and Jastin and Sajan were on a mission to track her down. They believed that she must have stolen Kirk's secret files before she phoned the Boston police and confessed to his murder. She had probably put them in a safe place somewhere because she would not have been dumb enough to try to hang onto them during her trial and her follow-up time in Witness Protection. The two Eckert brothers itched to get their hands on Kirk's documents in hopes of ferreting out information that would help them reestablish contact with the Russian agent to whom the Aryan Confederacy had paid two million dollars. But before the degraded fissionable material could be delivered by the Russian, the Aryan Confederacy compound had been destroyed, most of its cadre killed, and its founder, Conrad Pryzor, sent to prison, where he killed himself.

When Jastin parked the Blazer, he and Sajan got out, stunned and enraged by all the devastation. All the buildings, including the chapel, the mess hall, the headquarters, and the barracks, had been burned to the ground. Then the ashes and charred timbers had been carted away, leaving nothing but hard dirt, blackened concrete slabs, and utter desolation. They didn't stay long before Sajon said, "Let's get the fuck outta here, brother."

Their nostalgia for past glory turned to rage mixed with their memories of glory long gone. Their mom had brought them there when the place was thriving because she wanted both of her boys to get a well-disciplined upbringing. She had made up both of their names, Jastin and Sajan, right out of the top of her creative but somewhat addled mind, because she thought the unusual names would make them unique. Jastin was seven and Sajan was eight when she enrolled them in Conrad Pryzor's Aryan Youth Brigade, which was organized into troops, like the Boy Scouts or the Hitler Youth. As they progressed through its ranks from the Cub Platoon to the Bear Platoon and then to the Lion Platoon, they were methodically taught obedience and discipline, endurance and teamwork, stoicism and stealth. Eventually they learned jiu-jitsu, karate, and more lethal forms of hand-to-hand combat. By the time they were in their early teens they could assemble and disassemble the rifles and handguns that they used with extraordinary skill on the firing ranges. By age eighteen or nineteen, they were well-schooled in disguise and deception, escape and evasion, spy tactics, methods of sabotage, and assassination and murder.

Soon after their mother brought them there, they met and became close friends with Kirk Biggins, and the three of them went through all their training together. And they all excelled, not just in their formal pursuits within the Aryan Confederacy, but also in their extracurricular endeavors, one of which was to beat up and rob Jews and African Americans. They did it for spending money, but also for the thrills.

It was almost inevitable that when they drove away from the bare, burned-out grounds of the demolished compound they were itching for trouble. Any sort of "trouble" that would give them a taste of their "good old days."

They were on a dirt road not far from the old compound when they spotted a Black man on foot. "Let's git that nigger," Jastin said.

"Seig Heil!" Sajan said.

The Black man was walking at about eight o'clock on that Thursday night in June, coming from a family cookout down the road and heading for his own home which was about a mile and a half away. His name was Ephraim Jacobs and he was a stock boy at a Walmart, fifty-two years old. His mother was a kindergarten teacher and his father was an unpaid part-time preacher at a local Southern Baptist church with an all-Black congregation.

Ephraim quickly jumped to one side of the dirt road onto stubbly grass and tall weeds, where he wouldn't get hit by the approaching vehicle. But he didn't get out of the way fast enough, and Jastin hit him on purpose with the front end of the Blazer, not trying to run him over but just knock him down.

"What the hell!" Ephraim exclaimed, stifling a groan, and starting to get his legs under him as he tried to assess how badly he had been hurt.

59

But Jastin and Sajan leaped at him and pulled him all the way down. Then they kept hitting him in his face and head till he couldn't resist anymore and they were able to wrap him with ropes from the Blazer's cargo bay.

"Why you doin' this to me?" Ephraim mumbled weakly.

"We hate niggers," Sajan said.

He and Jastin picked Ephraim up after he was helplessly bound and dumped him into the cargo bay. Then Jastin hit the gas, spewing dirt under the tires so they could make a quick getaway. There wasn't likely to be any traffic at this time of night on the lonely dirt road, but they didn't want to take any chances.

The following morning, a White farmer, Elmer Corrigan, found the mutilated remains of Ephraim Jacobs in front of the Black people's church where Ephraim's father was the preacher. To Elmer, even though he was a humble farmer, not a crime scene investigator, it looked like Ephraim had been dragged to death by a thick rope, because some of its shredded coils remained under his arms and around his chest where the rest of it had been sliced off.

When the county sheriff, Sheriff Boyce, and his team of investigators arrived, they found blood tracks in the dirt showing that the decapitated man had been dragged for about three miles, and at roughly the halfway point of the dragging, his body must have hit a culvert because there were blood clots on the concrete, where his head and his right arm must have been severed and then deposited twenty and thirty feet away.

Although the coroner retrieved Ephraim's head, he couldn't identify him right away because his face, head and hair had been spray-painted silver, and then a swastika had been drawn on top of the silver paint when it must not have been all the way dry. It looked like the crude, smeary swastika had been made with a felt pen, maybe a Sharpie.

After the autopsy, the coroner told Sheriff Boyce that the dead man must have been conscious up till his head was torn off, because his brain and skull were intact. On the day after the autopsy, the victim was identified as Ephraim Jacobs after his name turned up in a missing persons report and his father was summoned to do the verification.

Sheriff Boyce persuaded FBI and government officials to designate the murder as a hate crime. A big shiny steel wrench was found with Ephraim Jacobs's blood on it, confirmed by a match to his DNA, so it seemed that at some point he must have been beaten with it. It was a Craft Master wrench with the name *Biggins* etched on it—which gave Sheriff Boyce a shock of recognition—but he knew that Kirk Biggins was shot to death by his wife, so he could not have been one of the perpetrators. However, one of the participants might have known Biggins while he was still alive.

Sheriff Boyce hoped that the bloody wrench might reveal a DNA mix from the victim and one of the perpetrators. He submitted the wrench to the FBI crime lab, hoping for a lucky break but doubting that he would get one.

CHAPTER 13

When my daughter, Joy, attempted to set up a meeting at the Southern Poverty Law Center in Atlanta, she was told that one of the SPLC's top investigators happened to be en route to Washington County, Pennsylvania, where a gruesome hate crime had been committed. Joy was momentarily taken aback by the coincidence that he was headed in *her* direction while she had thought she'd be headed to his.

"To whom am I speaking?" she asked the man on the phone.

"I'm Ari Applebaum, one of the lawyers here in our headquarters," he informed her. "I don't know when he'll be back. He booked an open-ended flight. But I can take a message and make sure he gets it."

"What happened that would make him fly here so suddenly?" Joy asked. "I'm phoning from Pittsburgh." She didn't say Clairton because most people would recognize the major city but not the small town.

"Well, you're close to where it happened," Attorney Applebaum said in a strained voice. "I happen to know that Washington, PA, is only about forty miles from Pittsburgh because that area used to be known as a hotbed of Klan and neo-Nazi activity, and now they might be rearing their ugly heads again—but we're hoping it might be an isolated incident, a lone wolf kind of thing."

"May I ask what you're referring to?" Joy inquired.

"Well, two days ago an innocent black man was dragged to his death on a dirt-and-gravel road about ten miles from the center of town. We thought the Aryan Confederacy was wiped out for all intents and purposes, but evidence was recovered that indicates that this latest atrocity might be the work of some of its renegades still alive and kicking and bent on revenge."

"The Aryan Confederacy is linked to a case we happen to be pursuing up here," Joy said. "I'm doing preliminary research and I thought that the ACLU and the SPLC were good places to start. But now, from what you're telling me, I should start closer to home."

"Unfortunately, that's probably true," Attorney Applebaum said.

When Joy got off the phone with the SPLC lawyer, she went into Vito's office to fill him in. "We have to go there," he said immediately. "If they've got something that implicates the Aryan Confederacy, I hope they won't hold back on us. We might have to tell them a few things about our case to nudge them into opening up. But we'll have to be careful not to bring any heat down on Roland Fornier."

"He's sure to *take* the heat if we leak anything about his granddaughter and he finds out about it," Joy said. "How soon do you want to go? I assume we'll be driving, not flying."

"You assume correctly," said Vito.

Joy phoned me to tell me they were going, but she knew I couldn't go with them because I had been tapped by a young filmmaker who had contacted me about doing a commentary track for a new DVD release of *Intensive Scare Part Three*, and I had agreed to be interviewed on camera at my home. I was glad to be able to bow out of the trip to Washington, Pennsylvania, because I always tried not to horn in on Joy's territory. She was the one working with Vito Martinelli on a day-to-day basis, not me, and I knew I had to grant her space. I couldn't help worrying about some of the potentially dangerous situations she might get herself into, but at the same time I couldn't impinge on her independence. The main source of conflict between me and my first wife was that she couldn't get it into her head that a parent's job is to raise a child who is capable of living on her own, not one who is *incapable* of doing that.

Ironically, while I was careful to let Joy spread her wings, she and her husband, Michael Bettinger, seemed to be having the same sort of dissention that had existed between her mother and me. I didn't dare ask Joy about it, but she eventually confided that Michael was dissatisfied with his own job and jealous of hers. In college, where they had met, they had both majored in journalism and hoped to become investigative reporters. After Michael graduated, a year ahead of Joy, he had landed an entry-level job with the *Pittsburgh Press* while Joy was finishing her senior year. Then she earned a master's degree and a doctorate while Michael worked hard to support them on his small salary and I helped out with monetary gifts usually disguised as birthday or Christmas presents, which he always thanked me for, but with a trace of resentment. He hadn't managed to rise above covering such things as garden shows and council meetings before the newspaper went out of business. Meantime Joy, who had taken advanced courses in criminology, had found her true calling when she started working for Vito. She was doing what she had always wanted to do, which was investigations, even though she wasn't writing them up or reporting on them on TV. Meantime, Michael was staying at home writing a novel and trying to find another job in journalism.

The novel he was writing was based on a screenplay he had written, which I had read. I tried to be gentle in my criticism of it, but it wasn't my cup of tea and I had no idea how I might help him get it financed. After all, I couldn't even get my own stuff green-lighted if it wasn't in the horror genre. And his screenplay and the novel based on it, of which I had read the first hundred and fifty pages, were laden with social commentary that made the dialogue sound too strident and too pedantic coming out of the mouths of his characters.

Joy was finding it increasingly difficult to deal with her husband's insecurities and his barely restrained anger that he was not succeeding as well as he wanted to.

Dissatisfied with his own status in life or his lack of noteworthy achievements, he often mocked or tried to horn in on hers. Therefore it did not surprise her, when she came home to pack an overnight bag for her trip with Vito, he wanted to pack a bag and go with her. .

"I could write a nonfiction book about the case you're working on," he said to Joy. "It might pave the way for my novel."

"My father will undoubtedly be writing that book," Joy told him as gently as she could. "He's got the reputation and the notoriety."

"And not *me!*" Michael said as his anger flared up. "You're my wife and you're supposed to *help* me! Do you think I like letting you be the breadwinner?"

"It's only temporary," she said. "You'll find something."

"Your father let me down!" he shot back at her. "He could've agreed to direct my screenplay, but he wouldn't do it! He gave me a mealy-mouthed runaround! He must be afraid that if he attached his name to something from me, it would hurt his reputation as the grand master of horror!"

"If you want to know the truth," Joy said, "he thinks your work is too esoteric, but he doesn't want to hurt your feelings."

Looking utterly distraught, Michael stomped into the little spare room that he used as his office and slammed the door. Joy thought about knocking lightly and letting herself in to apologize and soothe his feelings, but she forced herself not to. Instead she hurriedly packed her overnight bag and drove to Vito's house so they could both ride in his car to the scene of the hate crime they had just learned about. She was troubled that she and Michael had parted in anger, without so much as a hug or a kiss. She wished he would land a good-paying job that would give him a sense of dignity and refresh his belief in himself. She felt that in some ways he wanted to own her, yet he couldn't even feel worthy of her so long as she was the only one still bringing home a paycheck. She found herself recalling the snit he had thrown when she had chosen to stick to her birth name, Cristi, for professional purposes and to use the combination Bettinger-Cristi on their marriage license. She had hoped he would take it well, but he didn't. He said it made him feel belittled, even though she told him she didn't intend it that way. She was worried that they were headed for a divorce and might even be in the preliminary stages of a separation without wanting to realize it. She knew that her dad liked Michael even though Michael was so upset over the rejection of his screenplay. "Your father doesn't understand my kind of introspection and subtlety," Michael had griped to Joy as they lay in bed. "I really hate to say it but he's become too much of a Hollywood hack."

"Don't you put him down like that!" Joy had snapped indignantly. "My father happens to be one of the most insightful people I've ever known."

"Hmph!" Michael had snorted. "What am I? Chopped liver?"

They had turned away from each other and she had tried to get to sleep that night in spite of her worries about their relationship. She thought that her husband's ego needed some kind of a boost before it became incurably implacable. Underneath it all, he was a decent person but he couldn't handle rejection because he wasn't yet thick-skinned enough and that didn't bode well for survival in the dog eat dog entertainment business. He had to find some form of professional success or he would succumb to despair and defeatism.

What was the most troubling about all that was Joy's niggling fear that she had married someone who wasn't as strong and resilient as she had once believed. Truth be told, she had a sneaking suspicion that she was bolder than he was. When she had opened up about it to her father, he had urged her to stick with her husband and give him as much support as he needed. "He really does have a lot of talent," her father had insisted. "That's why I encouraged him not to stop writing, but keep on persevering and exploring in different idioms until he finds something that clicks. He took it the wrong way, as if I was putting him down, but if he thinks it over it's going to sink in. At least that's what I hope."

At this low moment in their marriage, Joy was wishing that she could trust her father's instincts and his well-meant words, but she was finding it difficult. Meantime, she couldn't let her personal situation affect her job. She didn't want to let Vito down. And she was deeply convinced that bringing Roland's case to a successful resolution might also deal a blow to the domestic terrorism that was a constant threat to the America she cherished. She realized that kind of high-minded thinking might sound silly to some people, so she didn't go around spouting it, but she quietly harbored it as one of her core beliefs.

CHAPTER 14

Joy and Vito met with an SPLC investigator, an ACLU investigator, and the sheriff of Washington County in the sheriff's office in Courthouse Square in the small, peaceful-seeming town of about thirteen-thousand people. The sheriff, who looked to be in his midforties, had dark brown hair and a thick mustache and was wearing a crisply starched tan and black uniform with gold collar insignia. The two African American men from the ACLU and the SPLC both looked to be in their late thirties or early forties, both clean-shaven and slightly balding and both wearing dark pinstriped suits with pastel neckties and pocket handkerchiefs—almost a standard uniform for lawyers.

After introducing them as John Luther from the ACLU and Mason Stuart from the SPLC, Sheriff Boyce revealed himself to be a history buff. "Our little town was the first one to be named after the Father of Our Country," he said with a touch of pride. "Our other claim to fame is that we're home to W&J—Washington and Jefferson college. Lots of people believe that George Washington slept here once during the Revolutionary War, which never actually happened. But when he became our first president, he ordered troops down here to quell an insurrection of moonshiners and moonshine lovers who despised a tax levied on alcohol by the federal government. That was the Whisky Rebellion. You might've heard of it."

"Yes, in one of my history classes," Joy said. "It seems like an anti-government sentiment goes way back around here."

"And still continuing, unfortunately," John Luther interjected.

"Thank *God* for the federal government!" Mason Stuart blurted stridently. "This country couldn't have survived very long under the Articles of Confederation. We desperately needed a strong central government."

Sheriff Boyce said to Vito and Joy, "John and Mason and I know each other very well. We helped government agents put an end to a plot concocted by the Aryan Confederacy back when they still had a lot of power. Conrad Pryzor, their leader at that time, came up with a scheme to get himself elected mayor, which he viewed as a steppingstone to the governorship of this entire state. It was a bizarre scheme that almost worked. He thought that if he could poison all the people who wanted to vote against him, he could win the election even though he didn't have majority support.

"You're kidding me," Vito said. "How could he have hoped to pull something like that off?"

"Well, it almost worked," John Luther retorted. "Pryzor's chemists incubated salmonella germs in their laboratory at the Aryan Confederacy compound. Then they sent out their minions to contaminate the salad bars and buffets in all the most popular restaurants. They figured that if they made enough people too sick to vote on Election Day, Conrad Pryzor would stand a great chance of winning. But their harebrained scheme was blown, thanks to a woman who hated her neo-Nazi husband and wanted him jailed."

"Instead, he was gunned down," Mason Stuart said. "FBI, SWAT teams, state troopers, and federal marshals surrounded the compound and most of the bastards were exterminated when they refused to surrender peacefully."

"Exterminated like the cockroaches they were," John Luther said, grimly reliving his own anger.

"Why did I never hear too much about it?" Vito asked. "The news releases I saw were very brief, and they downplayed everything, which must've been intentional."

"We had to keep a lid on it the best we could," Sheriff Boyce explained. "The Timothy McVeigh thing happened around that same time, and it immediately spawned copycats who got busy learning how to make bombs out of fertilizer. We didn't need to encourage the kinds of assholes who might want to create their own batches of salmonella poison. That was the last thing we wanted."

Joy had remained silent through this part of the discussion, letting Vito take the lead if and when he wanted to. During the drive down here, he had said, "Sometimes you have to give up a piece of yourself to get something back." She instantly understood what he meant because in her journalism courses her instructors had made her realize how devious she might have to be if she were to elicit meaningful tidbits of information from reluctant politicians. Likewise, Vito's strategy would be to try to get as much intel as possible from the sheriff and the men from the ACLU and SPLC, then try to pry even more out of them by opening up about the Fornier case only when it made good tactical sense to do so.

Meantime the conversation was interrupted when Sheriff Boyce's secretary brought in a tray laden with cups of black coffee along with cream, sugar, napkins, and stirrers and set it on an oaken side table so they could help themselves to the fixings.

When they were all seated and sipping, Mason Stuart said, "I was born and raised near here, and it galls me that this part of the state is notorious for Klan activity as if it were in the Deep South. I got my B.S. in political science from W&J and my law degree from Duquesne University, then I accepted a job with the Southern Poverty Law Center in Atlanta, the job I still hold. I

70

didn't want to work for a firm full of stuffed shirts. I wanted to do something relevant and important."

John Luther said, "Mason and I are cut from the same mold. Currently we're spending a lot of our time combating a neo-Nazi movement called White Power Acceleration. They believe that out-and-out terrorism is the best way to usher in the collapse of democracy so fascism can take its place."

"Hitler used his Brown Shirts in that same way," Joy said ruefully.

"You're a bright young girl," Mason said, and Joy took it in stride.

"I have to tell you fellows about our case," Vito said, deciding that this was the right moment to sum up what the Roland Fornier case was all about, from the shooting of Kirk Biggins in his bed by Roland's granddaughter to the withdrawal from the Witness Protection Program by Katherine and her daughter, Magda.

Everybody listened attentively, then Sheriff Boyce said, "We're all familiar with most of what you just told us, Vito, up to Katherine's trial and sentencing. Almost nothing involving neo-fascists ever gets by us. But once she went into the Program our records on her ended. Because the government made her disappear into thin air for all intents and purposes."

"Is there anything that connects the dragging death of your African American victim to the Aryan Confederacy?" Vito prodded.

"A slight connection...maybe," Sheriff Boyce said. "But it's not going to go anywhere that we can foresee. We found a large steel wrench with blood on it along with blood clots and clumps of skin and brain matter on that dirt road, and the thing is, the wrench must've belonged to Kirk Biggins at some point because his name is etched on it. But of course, he couldn't have been there when Ephraim Jacobs was tortured and killed so gruesomely, because Biggins has been long dead. If we could somehow figure out how someone else came into possession of Biggins's wrench, and who that someone else could be, then we'd have a great lead on one of the killers."

"What about DNA?" Vito asked.

"Being processed as we speak," the sheriff answered. "But I expect that the blood will have all come from Ephraim, and all of the partial fingerprints were too smudged to reveal any patterns or ridges."

"But there's still a smidgeon of hope for trace DNA," said John Luther.

"Well, fingerprints are made from oil on a person's fingers," said Vito. "So there might be a good chance for DNA, don't you think?"

"That's what we're hoping," said Sheriff Boyce. "But first it has to be extracted, and next it has to belong to someone in the data base. When and if we get to that point, we might get lucky since anybody capable of committing such an atrocious killing might already have a rap sheet and a saliva swab might have been taken in prison."

"Would it violate your protocol if you were to let me know how the DNA analysis turns out?" Vito asked.

"No, but it would violate the integrity of our investigation if you leaked it to the wrong people," the sheriff said. "For now let's be patient till the test results are in. As we go forward, I'll consider whether or not there's any way I can share information with you without jeopardizing our primary concern, which is to get justice for poor Mr. Jacobs."

CHAPTER 15

Unbeknownst to Vito and Joy, while they were meeting with Sheriff Boyce and the two investigators from the SPLC and the ACLU, Roland Fornier and Jocko Randolph had arrived at the scene of Ephraim Jacobs's dragging death. Roland was not the kind of man who would rely solely on a PI to delve into any circumstance that might have a bearing on his granddaughter's situation, and Jocko was extremely loyal to him in any of his undertakings.

Unknown to me or Joy or Vito at that time, Roland and Jocko did not buy into the salvage of a Spanish galleon's treasure solely with money they had earned from selling gambling machines to Native American casinos. The scuttlebutt about Roland being a hit man wasn't just empty rumor—truth be told, he and Jocko had occasionally pulled off those kinds of jobs, and Roland had rationalized that not only his youthful reputation as "that jailbird's son" but also his need to keep his kids safe from his nutty ex-wife had left him with few ways to earn any kind of honest living.

Over burgers and beers an hour ago, Roland and Jocko had alternately boasted, chuckled, or bitched about some of their illegal adventures. Indignantly calling to mind a crony who had botched a job he had delegated to him," Roland said to Jocko, "I paid him seven large up front and two days later he called me on my burner phone to say the job was done and he wanted the other eight, so naturally I asked him what he *broke,* and he said he didn't have to break *anything!*

Can you believe it? He claimed he didn't have to break anything 'cause the guy was a pushover. Lucky he wasn't in my presence or I would've choked him. I said, 'You fuckin' dumbass, you were supposed to *break* one of his arms or legs not leave him in one piece so he keeps on welching. If he doesn't pay up in a couple of days, I'm keeping the other eight thou that you were supposed to get.'"

"What a shithead," Jocko said. "Remember, I told you not to use him."

"I'm done with him," Roland said adamantly. "If he starts thinking about ratting me out after I don't give him any more money, I might have to put him in a ditch."

"I'll clear the table for you for half the bread," Jocko said with a grin and a chuckle. "Next time listen to me when I give you good advice."

Roland said, "Okay, so maybe I used the wrong guy for that strong-arm job, but it was peanuts compared to what we both pulled down for the hit-and-run we did on that chiseling pharmacist, and we couldn't have taken it if we didn't delegate that other little thing."

"True, true," Jocko said. "But let's pay the tab and get outta here."

That morning before breaking for lunch at the roadside diner, they had scrutinized all three miles of Ephraim Jacobs's dragging death, in hopes of spotting something the police might have overlooked. They had found traces of muddy gore and streaks of Ephraim's blood on the dirt-and-gravel road, and even more of it in the concrete culvert where his head and arm had been torn off. They had realized that there was plenty of evidence that would have helped detectives reconstruct the crime, but nothing that would help identify the murderers— unless there was something that law enforcement was holding back—which neither Roland nor Jocko had any way of knowing.

"We might have to bribe a county cop," Jocko suggested. "But we'd have to get ahold of the entire roster and dig into their backgrounds to figure out who to target."

"That's our big advantage over the cops," Roland said. "We can bribe people and they can't."

"Let's grab lunch, then come back," Jocko said.

Roland said, "Why? No new evidence is gonna drop out of the sky."

"Because we can bribe witnesses even easier than we can bribe the police. If we can find somebody who knows something they're withholding out of fear of the killers, a fistful of Ben Franklins might open them up."

"You've got a point," Roland admitted.

So they went back to the three-mile-long dirt road of a crime scene and started knocking on doors. Their expensive dress shoes were dusty from their previous exertions, but they still looked dapper in their silk neckties and smartly tailored three-piece suits since it was their habit to present themselves as if they were suave and prosperous-looking businessmen with no need to intimidate anybody.

But they got rebuffed by the few people who came to the front doors of the first three shabby farmhouses they approached, and no one answered when they knocked on the next five doors and there were no cars or trucks parked in the gravel driveways or weed-grown yards.

"This doesn't seem to be working," Jocko said.

"Let's try five or six more places before we give up," Roland said, doggedly determined.

"You wanna prolong the agony?" Jocko said tiredly.

The next two houses were a continuation of the futility. But at the one after that the door opened and they were greeted by an emaciated stooped-over old woman with a couple of dark moles on her face and oily looking gray hair coming loose from a straggly bun.

"Good afternoon, ma'am," Roland said to her. "We're investigating the death of Ephraim Jacobs, and we're hoping to find someone who may have spotted something unusual that night. Up till now we're severely stumped and we're looking for any kind of string we can pull on."

"String?" she said in a raspy and querulous tone of voice.

Roland explained, "Something to point us in the right direction, if possible. A clue, you might call it. It could be you saw or heard something that didn't seem worrisome at the time but could be more meaningful in retrospect."

Jocko butted in, saying, "My partner here talks too fancy at times, and I apologize for that. What he means is we're up a creek without a paddle unless we get help somehow. The kind of help that might open a path to justice for Mr. Jacobs."

"Well, my son Ralphie was acting mighty scared the morning right after that poor Black man got killed. I tried to git him to tell me what made him so antsy, but he wouldn't. Instead, he got hisself into a fight at the saloon where them bikers hang out in town, and I think he done it on purpose so he'd get thrown in jail for a while. I think he saw something that made him afraid. He used his one phone call to tell me he with his voice all shaky that he's wantin' to git bailed out and run away and hide somewheres, but Lord knows I don't have the fifteen hundred dollars."

"What's your boy's last name?" Roland asked.

"Ralphie Ingram. I'm his mom, like I said. I'm Molly Hester. Hester was the last name of my second husband."

"You don't have any idea what it was that had Ralphie so scared?" Jocko asked her.

"I take two sleeping pills afore I go to bed, even though I'm s'posed to take just one," Molly Hester said. "I need my rest so I can't let my arthritis keep me awake from pain, so I knock myself out and if a choo-choo thundered right through this house with its whistle blowin' I wouldn't stir."

76

"Well, thank you kindly, ma'am," Roland told her. "I think we might be able to help your son if he helps us in return."

"Don't you two git him in any worse trouble than he's already in," Mrs. Hester said in her scratchy voice. "There's worse ways to die than bein' dragged to death, and he knows it."

As she shut her warped front door with gray paint peeling off of it, Roland and Jocko stepped down off of her rickety porch and Jocko said, "Well, Roland, what's our next move and how're we gonna play it without getting detained by the police?"

"A plan's already taking shape in my brain," Roland answered. "I'll explain it to you while we hike back up the road to my car."

Their first step was to connect with a lawyer in town, and they did that by finding the not so prosperous-looking legal establishment of Attorney Richard S. Bassett, which was in a storefront on Main Street. In his dumpy little office with the door shut so his secretary couldn't hear them, they told the attorney, who was a bald and sickly looking middle-aged man wearing a cheap off-the-rack brown suit, that they wanted to give him five thousand dollars in cash to pay Ralphie Ingram's fifteen-hundred-dollar bail then keep the rest of the money for himself.

"Why don't you just pay the bail money yourself and not owe me anything," Attorney Bassett suspiciously asked.

"Because we have good reason not to draw the sheriff's attention to ourselves," Roland answered. "You just need to tell Mr. Ingram that the money is coming from two private eyes that want to talk with him on the up-and-up. We happen to know he needs cash to pull off a disappearing act, so he'll probably jump at the chance to get himself a bunch of money. So you out to find it easy to get him to do it. I'm sure you're a slick talker."

"I like to think that I am," Attorney Bassett said shamelessly.

Within the next couple of hours Bassett became over three thousand dollars richer when he delivered Ralphie Ingram to Roland and Jocko, both of whom were sitting in the front seat of

Roland's car which was parked in a vacant lot right across from the jail. They were tensed up, prepared to chase Ralphie down, but as Attorney Bassette departed, Ralphie meekly but hesitantly got into the back seat.

Roland said to Ralphie, "We're private investigators. You don't have to know our names, but we spoke to your mother, so we know you must have seen or heard something that might be a clue to the murderers of Mr. Jacobs. You tell us what that something is, and we let you go free. We'll even take you to the Greyhound bus station so you can get wherever you want to go real quick. We don't even want to know where that is."

Ralphie was silent for a long time. Then he said, "I'm s'posed to believe you're on the level? Maybe you're setting me up. Maybe I tell you what you want to know, then I don't live long enough to get on a bus."

Jocko said, "Give him the money, Roland. Maybe once he has it and likes the look and feel of it he'll decide to trust us. It seems to me he has no choice. He wouldn't be the first guy not to survive very long in a cell. So who're you gonna trust more, Ralphie? Us or the jailers? It's not unusual for jailers to take bribes. They might get their palms greased so you can be found hanging from the bars of your cell with your T-shirt wrapped around your neck."

Ralphie gave it some long moments of thought. Then he said, "I'm not sure which way to jump. But I guess I gotta trust *you* guys."

At that auspicious moment, Roland handed over a business-size envelope filled with cash, and Ralphie's eyes gleamed when he rifled through it as if he had never seen or felt that much money in his entire life. He took out an old beat-up wallet and put a small stack of bills into it, then stuffed the envelope containing most of the money inside his dirty plaid shirt.

"I didn't see all that much," he said. "But it was enough to rattle the hell outta me. It was a white truck with a Confederate flag on the bumper and a swastika in the back window of the cab, and I never got a good look at who was in there—but I damn well knew who it was—even though I was peeking out of the living room window, trying to make out what they were pullin' behind 'em that was bouncin' and bumpin' through a cloud of dirt, gravel and dust. It went by in only a couple of seconds and I almost fell down 'cause I was shakin' all over."

"Who was in the cab of that truck, and what kind of vehicle was it?" Roland asked.

"Like I said, I didn't get a good look, but I almost didn't need to. It was decked out with that Nazi kinda shit. And there's two nasty badass brothers that go around in a white Blazer like that. I seen 'em lotsa times in The Kickstand, a biker bar they hang out in, and so do I, 'cause I like to look at all the Harleys parked in front. Everybody is scared shitless of 'em."

"So what are their names?" Rolandasked, sounding offhanded and barely interested.

"Jastin and Sajan Eckert. They don't make no secret of the fact that they used to belong to that Aryan Confederacy outfit before it got demolished by the feds. But maybe they're just lyin'. Because why weren't they arrested by now?"

"Maybe because there's nobody who will testify against them," Jocko surmised.

"Where do you think they'd be hiding out?" Roland asked.

"I got no idea. But the cops could find out, couldn't they? They'd probably run their license plate and put out a whatchamacallit."

"A BOLO. Be On the Lookout," Jocko said.

"Yeah, that's it," Ralphie said, bumping his forehead with the palm of his hand. "I'm gonna be long gone now, hopin' they ain't gonna find me."

He eyed Roland and Jocko suspiciously.

"We won't rat you out," Roland assured him.

79

CHAPTER 16

On weekdays, Sarah Jamison, nee Katherine Fornier, got out of bed at seven a.m., made hot oatmeal or something equally nutritious for her six-year-old daughter, Laura, then dropped her off at Happy Bear Day Care, three miles away, before going to her job at Gilmore Associates, where she lost herself in the often madding details of doing people's taxes, which she didn't find maddening a lot of the time because they made her get so absorbed in dollars and numbers and complicated calculations that she could numb herself to her sad and scary past.

But this was a Saturday. She took Laura to Philadelphia's Natural History Museum, where Laura became awed and fascinated by the huge dinosaur skeletons and the realistic way that artists' re-imaginings of the extinct beasts roared and fought each other and devoured lesser creatures, which was implied, not shown in gory detail, on a resplendent Imax screen, then Sarah bought her a *Jurassic Coloring Book* she could barely wait to read and color in with her fresh pack of new crayons.

After, they were in the park and playground adjacent to the children's wing of the museum, and Laura was riding one of the plastic stegosauruses bouncing on steel springs. Sarah remembered doing that herself when she was little, except the thing she rode was a pony and she had begged her grandfather to put a quarter in the coin box that made the thing work. These days it seemed unreal to her that she had once shared with her grandfather the idyllic kinds of things she and Laura were sharing now.

He was really a kind and decent man, she thought. Tears rolled from her eyes and she started to rummage in her purse for a hanky when Laura ran up to her with a worried look on her little face and said, "Don't cry, Mommy. I'll kiss and make it better."

"It's all right, honey," Sarah said as her little daughter climbed into her lap. "I was just thinking about somebody I haven't seen in a long time."

Suddenly scared, Laura stiffened and pulled away, saying, "Is he…"

"No, he's not dead," Sarah said quickly even though she wasn't completely sure. "He's alive and in good shape for his age. Very good shape in fact…he's your grandfather…your great-grandfather, honey."

"How come I don't know him?"

"Maybe you will someday. Would you like to meet him?"

"I guess so," Laura said perfunctorily. "But I wanna color now, Mommy! And you can color with me! *Please!*"

"Okay. Let's sit at that picnic bench."

Sarah and Laura got the coloring book and the package of new crayons out of the plastic dinosaur bag, then they picked two pages that they opened and flattened, a tyrannosaurus on the left page and a brontosaurus on the right, and they chose crayons and started coloring. Sarah refrained from correcting Laura for choosing purple for her dinosaur. She wondered if she was a good mother, because her own mother had died giving birth to her, and she had never had her for a role model. She had never known her father either. Maybe that's why she had made some big, stupid mistakes as a teenager.

She realized that her grandfather had tried hard. He had always been honest with her. Anytime she got curious about something, she could depend on him to answer her questions as well as he could. He had told her why her mother had died and

81

that her biological father was too young and wild to raise her properly.

Sarah wished that her own daughter could have a male role model in her life who would counteract the damage done by her biological father, Kirk Biggins. This made her wonder for the thousandth time if some kind of reunion with the grandfather who had raised her might someday be possible.

CHAPTER 17

Joy phoned me from Vito's office, her voice tense. "Dad," she said anxiously, "Sheriff Boyce was here for the past two hours with one of his deputies. They just left. I don't know if they're on their way to question you, but let us know if they do."

"Question me about what?"

"They found a burned-out vehicle yesterday with two bodies in it."

Vito's voice came at me from the land-line extension on his desk. "Two crispy critters," he said with his usual imperviousness. "In a Chevy Blazer or what was left of it, mostly black, twisted metal. But they got the VIN number and ran it and it was registered to a former Aryan Confederacy asshole with a helluva rap sheet—name of Justin Eckert. They figure the other crispy critter must be his brother, Sajan—two ugly peas in a pod. Somebody must've fingered 'em for what they did or were thought to have done to that Black man down there."

"Ephraim Jacobs," I reminded him.

"Yeah, I know. Joy and I were grilled separately at first, and we had a hard time for a while, but I think at bottom, the sheriff didn't think we were viable suspects. We drove straight home right after we left his office, and I was able to show him time-stamped receipts from the gas station we stopped at."

"Why would Joy think I was next on their list? I can prove I was here all day yesterday doing a commentary track for my movie sequel."

"I wanted you to be forewarned just in case," Joy interjected.

And Vito said, "Sheriff Boyce is trying to dot the i's and cross the t's like any good lawman would. We were totally honest with him and clued him in that the Roland Fornier case came to us through you. So he wants to clear you as a person of interest."

I said, "Who do you really think killed those two bastards?"

Joy said, "Vito and I think someone believed, rightly or wrongly, that the Eckert brothers must have tortured and killed Ephraim Jacobs. It's a wonder they weren't dragged to death by a rope or chain behind their own vehicle. Because for them to end up the way they did, and so soon, is too much of a coincidence."

"Well, I agree," I had to tell them. "I certainly hope Roland Fornier is in the clear. I hate to even think that way, but I guess we have to. If it's found out that he and Jocko are operating under a black flag, suspicion is going to fall on us as well."

"I got on the phone with Roland just as Joy was calling you," Vito said. "I didn't talk with him for very long because he immediately said that he and Jocko were at the Meadows racetrack all day yesterday and he had betting stubs to prove it. He didn't seem to take any offense at anything I asked him. But he did say he hopes the Eckert brothers are burning in hell."

"I'm not surprised he would say something like that," I said. "And I don't blame him. But racetrack stubs aren't too hard to get."

"My thoughts exactly," Vito said. "And of course I don't think Sheriff Boyce would be too persuaded by them. Because neither am I. Are you, David?"

"Nope."

None of us said it out loud, but the rumors about Roland operating as an occasional hit man had to cross each of our minds. What type of client did we have? How hard should we push him to tell us the truth, one way or the other? And should we drop the case if we couldn't fully trust him? I didn't want to lose him as a lifelong friend. Nor did I wish to abandon him when he needed my help, especially if he hadn't killed anybody.

Joy summed up our unspoken thoughts when she said, "I hope we can quickly find Roland's granddaughter, reunite them, and extract ourselves from this whole situation."

"Amen," I responded.

Vito said, "Knock on wood." And I could picture him rapping his knuckles on his forehead.

CHAPTER 18

I mostly didn't tend to believe that Sheriff Boyce and his deputy would show up at my house, but they did, and at first I put it down to the fact that there were plenty of times when people were motivated by a chance to meet me. Most people wouldn't tend to think it would apply to a police officer, but I had learned that even they weren't immune to celebrity. It was my habit, when some of my fans got all flustered in my presence, to say to them that I put my pants on one leg at a time like everyone else.

Diane was having lunch and then was going shopping with Vito's wife, Donna, and I was by myself. I was reading a James Lee Burke novel—one of my absolute favorite authors—and enjoying a day of peace, totally to myself, after having to be psyched up the day before to come off well on my commentary track for *Intensive Scare Part Three*. The interviewer had said at the wrap-up, "You're probably going to be one of these guys who ends up being carried off of a movie set."

And my retort was, "Hey, you can relax when you're dead— it even gets easier." Which I thought was a pretty good closer. But that self-congratulatory thought was interrupted by the ringing of the doorbell, and sure enough the sheriff and the deputy were on the front porch.

I let them in graciously, and they introduced themselves. I already knew the sheriff's name, but he said it anyway and we shook hands, then he introduced Deputy Mathis. I ushered them into the living room and got them seated, then offered them coffee but they protested that they were coffeed out.

Sheriff Boyce said, "We just have a few questions since we already know that you brought a certain case to Vito Martinelli and it caused them to come to my office yesterday out of the blue."

"Yes," I admitted. "My pal, who I grew up with, Roland Fornier, needs help finding his granddaughter and her child, and I recommended Vito. My daughter, Joy, works for Vito so they keep me in the loop. Other than that, I don't know any more than they do, and probably a lot less. I don't stay actively involved."

"But you've been involved a lot more than that in some of his other cases, and you've made a lot of money writing about them."

"Maybe not as much money as one would think," I said to him. "But that's neither here nor there."

"No, I guess it isn't," the sheriff acknowledged. "But what *is* germane, or at least seems to be, is that Mr. Martinelli and your daughter came to my jurisdiction sticking their noses into a vicious murder, then two persons of interest were found dead and incinerated inside a burned-up vehicle that belonged to one of them."

"My daughter wouldn't ever have been part of anything like that," I stated adamantly.

"But Vito would?" Deputy Mathis shot back at me.

The sheriff shot him a look that meant he wasn't to ask any questions until he was given the go-ahead to do so.

The deputy clammed up and Sheriff Boyce said, "Did your pal the *private investigator* tell you everything they did and everybody they might've spoken to when they came down to my crime scene?"

I thought about his question for a long pause. Then I said, "I couldn't testify that they told me all of it, but they certainly gave me what I thought was a full report." Tongue in cheek, I added, "If they killed anybody, they failed to mention it."

Well, all right, I was being flippant. But the sheriff wasn't about to let me get away with it. "You better not even think about obstructing justice," he warned me, "because you won't be making any more of your bloody movies if I put you behind bars."

I promptly apologized for being a jerk, then I said, "I really don't know whether or not Vito and Joy found any suspects down there, and I don't think they would have murdered them if they got a chance. Somebody else has to have done it."

"Any idea who?" Sheriff Boyce asked immediately.

I decided to keep Roland Fornier and Jocko Randolph out of it, telling myself rather handily that I had no real grounds for suspecting them. Which was mostly true. So it was easy to believe I had no right to bring any heat down on them. And I hoped that belief would never come unglued.

CHAPTER 19

Vito got in touch with Roland Fornier and arranged another get-together at the King's Castle. There were five of us because Roland wanted Jocko Randolph to be there, and Joy and I rounded out the group. Vito, as well as Joy and I, had also wanted Jocko to be there but Vito hadn't wanted to make it obvious that he was glad it had worked out that way. If either Jocko or Roland had anything to do with the "crispy critters" in the burned-out Blazer, we hoped one of them would slip up.

To come off as disarmingly as I could while we waited for our first round of drinks, I reminisced good-naturedly with Jocko by joshing him about the first time I went to his house to work out with him. First, I helped him haul about four hundred pounds of barbell and dumbbell plates and bars up from his basement and into his little backyard. Then we each grabbed opposite ends of his heavy workout bench and carried it up. Then he told me we needed to lug all of it to the playground, which was two blocks away. And when I asked why we couldn't just work out right there in his yard, he said, "You'll see. It's a lot better to do it in the playground." Well, huffing, puffing and sweating from "pumping iron" by trundling it, I saw why he said it would be "better" to work out at the playground—because the luscious playground supervisor was a nineteen-year-old girl in a red halter that barely encased her breasts and red short shorts that revealed the bottoms of her voluptuous buttocks—and Jocko unabashedly had the screaming hots for her. My telling of this story made everybody laugh, and Jocko laughed too, not even turning the least bit red.

"I never got anywhere with her," he said. "She wouldn't have gone out with me if I was Arnold Schwarzenegger. She had a boyfriend her own age who was a skinny little shit with a face full of puss-oozing pimples."

"Was he tall?" Roland said. "Because tall skinny kids have big penises. Sorry, Joy."

But she was chuckling so he laughed too.

The drinks came and after that Vito bridged into the serious part of the meeting by giving a report on the trip that he and Joy had made to Little Washington and summing up what they had learned from the sheriff and from people who lived at or near the crime scene. When he finished his spiel nobody else piped up even though this was when Roland or Jocko should've mentioned that they also were down there.

Vito, Joy, and I held back, even as our suspicions heightened. And Roland must have sensed this, because he said, "I don't want there to be any secrets among us because that would certainly be counterproductive. I was meaning to tell all of you that Jocko and I did take a sort of spontaneous drive to look for ourselves along that dirt road to see if we might spot something that was missed. And we talked to an old woman who told us that her son was making her think he saw something, but we couldn't find him where she said he always hung out, so we left. I'd like to give you his name, Vito, so you can turn it over to the sheriff. Who knows what might come of it?"

"Yeah, I'd appreciate having that name so Joy and I can do follow-up," Vito said. He kept his facial expression placid, a poker face, like the investigator that he was, not about to betray his feelings.

But Roland said, "You act like you don't believe me."

But Jocko cut in, saying, "C'mon, man, he's a former cop and his old habits aren't gonna die because now he's a private cop. He trusts nobody. Which is as it should be."

"Yeah, you're right, Jocko," Roland admitted.

"However," said Vito, "I'd appreciate it if you'd leave the investigating to me—and Joy. You're paying us, that's true, but the client shouldn't step on the investigator's toes."

"We won't do it anymore," Jocko said, by way of instantly voicing compliance for both himself and Roland.

"I stand chastened," Roland said with a self-deprecating smile.

"Okay," said Vito. "Let's move forward. I wish there was some way we could find out a helluva lot more about the two bastards who must have been killed because someone knew or believed they knew that they were the ones responsible for the dragging death of that Black man."

"I can get into their criminal records online," Joy told us. "It's also easy enough to find out their family histories and so on. But what we really need to know is who their pals are. How did they get that wrench with Kirk Biggins's name etched on it, if we assume they got it somewhere? Who could've owned it before they did, other than Biggins?"

"Right on," said Roland. "Because birds of a feather flock together. They all knew each other because they were all part of the Aryan Confederacy. It follows that Jastin and Sajan had to be done in before they could rat other members out. Maybe motherfuckers unknown were helping Kirk Biggins build his uranium bombs. And maybe they're still at it now that Kirk is dead."

"That's a good point," I said. "It's one that Vito and Joy and I already thought of, and it gives us our best direction to go in. We have to discover who cremated the two Eckert brothers in their own SUV."

"Well, we'll leave you to it," Roland said. "We won't interfere anymore, I promise. Jocko and I will be on our way. We've got other important concerns anyhow. We're fighting with our treasure-hunting syndicate members over what our share is gonna be."

We shook hands all around and Roland bussed Joy on her cheek which made her smile uneasily. None of us wanted to betray our concern about how Roland and Jocko knew the names of the Eckert brothers when neither Vito nor Joy nor I had mentioned them by name.

After Roland and Jocko left the King's Castle I said, "Suppose if worse comes to worst it gets more likely than not that Roland and Jocko snuffed the Eckert brothers out. That would mean they would've grilled them first, probably even tortured them. They might've gotten some kind of lead that they're keeping from us and are probably gonna act on."

"And, Dad, you don't want to have to think that way," Joy said, reaching out and nudging my face.

"But I know I have to be objective, no matter what comes up," I said grimly.

"I'm asking myself how much I care so long as they kill the right people," Vito admitted. "And as far as you're concerned, Dave, lots of people already think you don't have any scruples because of the kinds of movies you make. But are you really squeaky clean in your own mind?"

"Pure as the driven slush," I quipped. "But I don't think I'd be able to rat Roland out if I suspected or even knew for sure that he and Jocko took the law into their own hands against any of the bad guys we're either dealing with already or that we might eventually close in on."

CHAPTER 20

Todd Nalepka, who dressed like a smart, successful businessman most of the time, except on nights when he wore his leathers and exposed his plethora of Satanic and Nazi tattoos at The Kick Stand, had laid low and stayed away from his favorite biker bar for two weeks because it looked to him like somebody was carrying out a vendetta against former Aryan Confederacy members wherever they could be found. The dead ones that he knew about so far were Leroy Hubbard and Jordan Giese in Philadelphia and Jastin and Sajan Eckert right here in southwestern Pennsylvania. His bosom buddy Kirk Biggins probably wasn't a casualty of the vendetta because his assassination was carried out by his own wife who was just a dumb crazy bitch with a hair up her ass. For a couple of years guys like Todd Nalepka were only half-heartedly pursued, probably thought to not even worth the trouble after most of the Aryan Militia was massacred and their compound was demolished and razed to the ground by the feds.

Nalepka didn't like to admit that he was afraid of anybody or anything, including any kind of wacky conspiracy against him and his pals. In his own mind he was a *Natural Born Killer*. That smash-hit movie was almost the story of his life. Nobody better ever fuck with him. He was damn near seven feet tall and weighed close to three hundred pounds, yet he was broad at the shoulders and narrow at the hips due to his hours long workouts while staring admiringly at himself in the full-length mirrors at the Executive Health Club in the upscale mall on the outskirts of town, not far from his ritzy condo.

He was his own kind of man, and he liked the double life he led and how it enhanced his unique, unorthodox lifestyle. He couldn't envision ever departing from it. It kept him from being caught or even suspected. Gone forever were his days as a meek, self-hating crybaby.

His parents got divorced when he was two years old, then his mother married a brutal alcoholic who repeatedly molested him. Scared to tell on his stepfather, when he was in kindergarten, he was too small and meek to beat up other girls and boys so he went behind their backs to stomp on their toy cars and trucks and the towers they made out of Tinker Toys, leaving a mess of demolished toys. Sometimes he scrawled dirty words in the other kids' coloring books without getting caught. At age seven he shot a neighbor's dog's eyes out with a BB gun and killed his mother's goldfish by pouring Drano in their aquarium. He spent three months in a psychiatric hospital because of his inability to control his rage against teachers and guidance counselors.

From twelve years old on up, he was forced to work in his stepfather's meat packing plant, where he got transformed from a skinny little sneak to a heavily muscled bully by long hours spent dragging and hoisting beef and pork carcasses. With his newfound strength and arrogance, he started slapping his mother around just like his stepfather did. Deathly afraid of him, she gave up on him and sent him to live with his biological father. That got him away from his sexually perverted stepfather, whom he was secretly thinking about killing. His mother either never got wise to what was going on behind her back or else she repressed it.

While living in a ramshackle house on his father's small decrepit farm, he was allowed to shoot rabbits and deer with pistols, rifles, and shotguns. A hardened criminal who had done several short stints in prison, Todd's father sometimes brought him along on burglaries or smash-and-grab jobs or used him as a lookout on armed robberies and also taught him how to make homemade pipe bombs and use them to blow up tree stumps and stacks of rocks, which was the beginning of a fascination with explosives that later made him a close buddy of Kirk Biggins.

In the meantime, Todd's latent inclination toward lechery reemerged, and at age fifteen he kidnapped a fourteen-year-old girl who was one of his high school classmates. Menacing her with a .22-caliber revolver, he kidnapped her and forced her into the woods where he tied her up, taped her mouth shut, and raped her. Then he walked her home as if they had been on a date, all the while threatening to kill her brother and sister if she told on him. But she told anyway, and he was tried as an adult and sentenced to fifteen years in prison. The judge had assessed him to be very bright academically but so behaviorally and emotionally dangerous he probably could not be rehabilitated.

In May of 2001 Todd was released from prison, as a registered sex offender, on good behavior after serving fourteen years. He moved to Columbia where his mother was living but did not move in with her. She had told his parole officer that she didn't want him to move in with her since she was still terribly afraid of him. But he fooled others into thinking he was rehabilitated because while he was in prison, he had gotten an online college degree in computer science. This enabled him to go to work for a small website design firm and, and operating under the terms of his employment contract, they paid half of the costs of his Bachelor of Science degree in business administration and marketing.

Because of the degrees he had earned, in spite of being a registered sex offender, he was able to obtain a real estate license and eventually start his own firm with a half dozen agents in his employ, and by and by he became quite wealthy. At this point his twisted self-confidence exploded. He bragged about his rank as a top seller. He boasted to colleagues about his firearms collection and the things he liked to do to women who fell under his control. Several young women in his employ left his company because it alarmed them that he watched pornographic videos at his desk and didn't shut them off when they entered.

But if he raped or killed any young women during this time, he did not come under any suspicion. He kept on masquerading as a wealthy and successful businessman. He did not let it be known that he was a supporter and major contributor to Conrad Pryzor's Aryan Confederacy. And he maintained contact with some of the survivors of the raid just outside of Washington, Pennsylvania that put an end to Pryzor and all that he had built up.

Then a dispute between Todd Nalepka and a store called Superbike Motorsports took a bad turn and the owner, the manager, a mechanic, and a bookkeeper were shot dead. Todd was the leading suspect even though there wasn't any evidence against him, except that the owner's widow said he had threatened to blow the place apart when they refused to compensate him for damages to a Harley he had bought and wrecked, because they had brushed him off, saying the accident was his fault for not knowing how to ride one properly. He eluded arrest but was often spotted on his Harley in fields and on dirt roads, practicing so he could become a highly skilled biker. He did not want to be a mere biker wannabe. But he still wanted to preserve his image as a dignified, highly affluent businessman, which was why he "dressed biker" when he was at The Kickstand but "dressed normal" when he wasn't.

But now he felt like he was walking around with a target on his back. He desperately needed to find out who had killed his pals and might soon be coming after him. He was a big strong guy underneath his expensive suits, but neither a three-piece suit nor a biker's leathers would stop a bullet. And bullets could take a person down in a sudden blast from any good hiding place.

Todd had been one of the main financiers of Kirk Biggins's uranium bomb planting scheme prior to Kirk's unfortunate death, so Todd's hatred of Katherine Biggins was not only palpable but like an eternal flame that could never be tamped down or stamped out. He wanted to avenge Kirk and finish what Kirk had started, and he felt strongly, or wanted to believe in the possibility that Katherine had stolen Kirk's plans.

But she was in Witness Protection where she couldn't be touched.

Or could she?

Money was not just the root of all evil, it was the reliable means by which almost all honest people could be corrupted, even lawmen who had started out on a straight-and-narrow path or politicians who had been honorable throughout their careers. Until the worm turned.

Todd had plenty of money. He needed to find the right person to bribe. A United States Marshal working inside the Witness Protection Program would be ideal because Todd could pay him or her more in one day than they ever had earned in any given year.

But how could he latch on to the perfect palm to be greased? He couldn't hope to find out where the Program had relocated Katherine and her child or what names they might be using now.

Then he recalled that two US Marshals had escorted Katherine Biggins out of the courtroom after she stepped down from the witness stand. Perhaps he could dredge up some news footage that would grant a clear image of their faces. And from there, if he got lucky, he might be able to zero in on who they were and where they were based. Then he could use his money to loosen their tongues. Not necessarily both of them, but at least one—one corruptible United States Marshal.

Todd Nalepka believed that every person on earth was dishonest for a price. Just like that old joke where a guy asks a gal if she would go down on him for a million bucks and she turns red but thinks about it and says that a million bucks would tempt her. So he says, "What about for five bucks?"

And she snaps, "What do you think I am—a prostitute?"

97

He says, "We've already established that. Now we're negotiating."

There was a piece of business he had to take care of before he could totally concentrate on finding Katherine Biggins. So he had the Big Breakfast right off of the glossy photographic menu of a place *called* The Big Breakfast, then he drove his pickup truck out to a hundred-acre piece of property that he owned, thirty-some miles from his condo. It was empty weed-grown land that he paid a farmer to keep mowed, except a sixty-by-eighty section was fenced in around a trailer and a large steel storage container like the ones used to transport trade goods on ships. It was where he had locked up the waitress from The Big Breakfast who had complained about the sexual innuendos and pats on her nice ass that he had laid on her when she served him. She had almost gotten him banned from the place, but she had dropped her complaint after he offered her and her boyfriend a hundred bucks a week to take over the farmer's job of keeping the property mowed.

He had killed her boyfriend, of course. Then he had turned her into his sex slave, keeping her locked up for the past several weeks in the steel storage container which he had soundproofed beforehand. It was a lovely arrangement for him. The boyfriend was buried in a patch of woods far away and she was available anytime he felt the need. He hated to give her up. But the police had questioned him several times, making him feel a bit too threatened.

He pulled his truck up close, then unlocked her "cell" and let her out. She was so meek and subdued by now that he didn't even have to prod her with his pistol. As a treat to himself he had his way with her on a foam mattress in his nice clean trailer instead of on the old quilt on the floor of the container. He told her, "This will be our last time together. Then I'm going to set you free." She probably wasn't burned-out enough to believe him, but he didn't care.

After their delightful little interlude, he strangled her, then wrapped her body in a blanket, loaded her into the bed of his pickup and drove her to where he had buried her boyfriend. He put her next to him in a freshly dug grave so they could spend eternity together. He grinned as he said a short prayer over them, "Ashes to ashes, dust to dust," amusing himself by mumbling it.

He really did not think there was anything sacred about the human body. It was nothing more than a sack; ugly and containing a mess of organs and viscera. A major portion of the sack was taken up by a large intestine full of feces and so, to a large extent the derisive comment "you sack of shit" was accurate. That thought made Todd chuckle. If you stabbed someone forty or fifty times all you were doing was puncturing the sack of shit over and over, thereby making total decomposition easier and faster. The maggots liked it that way.

The human body was *composed* of…and then it was *de*composed. But yet Todd *liked* the feel of human bodies while they were warm and alive. He wasn't a necrophiliac and thought himself superior to those who were. He liked male and female bodies indiscriminately, with a preference for pre-teen girls and boys. To him there was no reason for discrimination according to sex. Kids all felt the same, smelled the same, etcetera, regardless of gender.

As he got back into his truck and drove away from his most recently created burial site, he let his mind wander. He realized that little Magda Biggins must be six or seven by now. Perfect. He did yet know what kind of surname she might have been given when she was taken by her mother into Witness Protection, but he was fairly confident he would soon find out.

The quest for a continuation of the fissionable bomb plans and the needed materials almost took second place in his own mind, although it certainly was a quite worthwhile goal in an intellectual sense. And Todd considered himself an intellectual, hardly on an equal plane with the dumb brutes who did brutal grunt work for the Aryan Confederacy. They were akin to Adolf Hitler's Brown Shirts. No brains, just brawn—cattle for the cause to be used and then enslaved or eliminated after they had served their purpose.

Todd Nalepka had always felt that he and Kirk Biggins were soul mates in a sense, even though he didn't believe that anybody on this earth actually had a soul. He and Kirk had the same kinds of sexual urges, and with no shame attached. They fervently believed that they were superior beings, not just superior to the "mud races" but even superior to other Aryan leaders due to their high IQ's and their dedication to scientific endeavors that could only have been matched by Adolf Mengele, the Grand Experimenter at Auschwitz who was derogatorily labeled a Doctor of Death by the allied invaders who had called themselves "liberators." Mengele was forced to flee to Argentina, abandoning his ground-breaking experiments on Jews and gypsies. One of his most daring and innovative procedures was injecting children's eyes with radical new dyes that would turn their eyes blue, thus rendering them more acceptable for adoption by Aryan couples in the Thousand Year Reich that Adolf Hitler envisioned.

Todd had little doubt that if Kirk Biggins's crazy wife hadn't killed him, he and Kirk would have achieved great things as scientific colleagues and the Thousand Year Reich would have been a dream come true. He was obsessively determined to carry the Fuhrer's glorious vision to fruition and bring the Aryan Race to supreme power over the Deep State that thus far had perversely and smugly ruled this degenerate twentieth century.

He worked days on end at his computer, often going without sleep for over twenty-four hours at a stint, searching for a face of a United States Marshal that he might recognize from coverage of Katherine Biggins's trial. That was the first step, he kept telling himself; first zero in on a prospect; then probe into the prospect's past and present to ascertain whether or not he or she might be corruptible. Todd Nalepka knew as the result of his many successes in bribery, not to mention the pervasive corruption in today's degenerate society, that most people would bend or subvert their lifelong morals and principles for the right price.

Finally, on the eighth or ninth sleepless day of his computer search, he recognized a face that he had found in dredged-up news footage.

CHAPTER 21

Totally ignorant that Todd Nalepka was lurking in the nebulous intertwinements of the Roland Fornier case, Vito, Joy, and I met in Vito's conference room in the early morning of July second. Our purpose was to fathom a logical way to go forward. We were all wearing casual clothing, T-shirts, cutoff jeans, and sneakers, because after our meeting we were headed to a pre-Fourth of July cookout at Vito's place but we felt like we should do some work first

None of us had a specific idea of what our next move should be, so Joy suggested we put together a chronology of what had taken place so far—or what we knew had taken place so far—in hopes that in doing so things would come into sharper focus and generate some kind of inspiration.

The result of our brainstorming was the following, typed up by Joy on her laptop and printed out at the office:

- David Cristi gets his first phone call from Roland Fornier and they meet that day at The Interchange where David learns that Katherine Biggins is Roland's granddaughter and she killed her abusive neo-Nazi husband, Kirk Biggins, before he could carry out his plot of planting dirty-uranium bombs. She went on trial and then was put into Witness Protection but absconded less than a year afterwards. . Roland wants to find her and protect her from any further harm from Kirk's buddies or anyone else.

- Vito agrees to take on Roland's case, and of course Joy, as his employee, will be a willingly helper, as will David, if need be.
- Meantime, Leroy Hubbard and Jordan Giese stalk and kill Judge Steingart. Giese is killed during the murder, and Hubbard kills himself when he gets surrounded by police—but just prior to his suicide, he murders the parents of Hayley Hunter while trying to hide in their home.
- David, Joy, and Vito meet up with Roland Fornier and Jocko Randolph at The King's Castle. Roland and Jocko have remained buddies all these years, did many adventurous things together like selling gambling machines to Native American casino operators and salvaging treasure from long-sunken Spanish galleons. Were they once hit men? Or are they still?
- Jastin and Sajan Eckert, members of the Aryan Confederacy right up to the time of their deaths, drag a black man named Ephraim to death outside of Washington, Pennsylvania, near where the Aryan Confederacy compound used to be. The two brothers are found incinerated in their own vehicle.

Joy and Vito go to Little Washington to meet up with Sheriff Boyce, John Luther (ACLU) and Mason Stuart (SPLC). Joy and Vito get details about the dragging death of Ephraim Jacobs, including the finding of the bloody wrench with Kirk Biggins' name on

- On the heels of finding the Eckert brothers incinerated, Sheriff Boyce and Deputy Mathis interrogate Vito, Dave, and Joy. The lawmen obviously suspect that

Roland and Jocko may have killed the Eckerts, and Vito, David, and Joy cannot rule out that possibility.

- Another meeting of Vito, Joy, and David with Roland and Jocko at The King's Castle. It's an uncomfortable get-together because Vito, Joy, and David don't want to betray their sneaking suspicion that Roland and Jocko might have killed the Eckerts.
- Morning of July Fourth—the latest meeting of Vito, David, and Joy about the whole mess. Created timeline of discovery thus far.

We brainstormed all those talking points over and over and over for the next hour and a half, without any resolution or any hard and fast plan ever materializing. By that time, we were all so weary of contemplation that we decided to just knock it off and relax enough to enjoy the cookout.

It was our vague hope that if we ingested some booze and pushed the investigation out of our minds for a while, one of us might be hit with sudden inspiration—like if you're trying to remember the title or tune of a song and it won't come to you in an instant when you're not trying too hard to latch on to it.

As Vito locked the front door to his office, I said, "Is it okay if I invite Roland and Jocko to your cookout if they happen to still be around?"

He said, "Sure, why not? Maybe if I bust their chops, they'll drop their guard and blurt something out."

I knew that he meant "bust their chops" figuratively, not literally, since he wouldn't want to start a brawl at his own picnic. At least I hoped he wouldn't. Back when he was on the local police force, he was accused more than once of being too rough with suspected criminals, either while arresting them or interrogating them. None of the accusations ever seemed to have stuck, but still I had to wonder if he had gotten his dark side under control or if it might flare up again.

CHAPTER 22

Todd Nalepka's long hours of grinding away at his computer till he almost believed his eyes would bleed and his fingers go numb finally paid off in the thrill of a eureka moment. He congratulated himself for his relentless adherence to his original plan. He had a doggedly clever Internet expertise and an utter lack of scruples that could have made him an extremely wealthy perpetrator of online schemes and scams if he hadn't chosen to become a real estate developer instead. His skills in the world of logins, electronic IDs, and passwords would always be his ace in the hole should he ever have a need to exploit them out of whim or necessity.

He had hacked into a government data base containing photo IDs, awards and citations, career histories and vital statistics of what looked to be a complete roster of the United States Marshals. This enabled him to find a facial match with a newsreel image of one of the two marshals who had been at Katherine Biggins's trial.

Ryan Burke was currently based out of the Alfred P. Murrah Federal Building in Oklahoma City—which gave Todd Nalepka a delicious thrill because it was the very building that had been truck-bombed by Timothy McVeigh in 1995 as an act of vengeance against ZOG—the Zionist Occupation Government of the United States.

Before Todd Nalepka boarded a plane for Oklahoma City, there was something bugging him that he wanted to take care of. Because his handyman and grass mower, Ralphie Ingram, had disappeared right when Jastin and Sajan Eckert were killed,

Todd suspected that perhaps Ralphie had fingered them. So he spiffed himself up in an expensive suit, vest and silk tie and went to visit Ralphie's mom, Mollie Hester. He knocked on the rickety front door and when it opened Mollie stepped onto the porch.

Todd said, "Good afternoon, ma'am. I wanted your son Ralphie to take care of my property for me while I go on a business trip, but he hasn't shown up so I'm hoping he's not ill or something."

"No, he's not sick, but he's not here," Mollie said in her raspy high-pitched voice. "He gave me a thousand dollars—I'll be darned if I can figure out where he got it—and he took a taxi to the airport. Wouldn't even tell me where he's headed or when he'll be back."

"How long ago did he leave?" Todd asked, trying to sound casual about it. "Yesterday maybe? That's when he didn't show up at my place. I remember because it was only a couple days before that those two young fellers were found all burned up."

Mollie tried to suppress a shudder and didn't succeed. Warily she said, "I sure hope you don't think my boy had anything to do with that."

"No, no, not at all. I just don't want to hire somebody else if Ralphie still wants the job."

"I don't see how he can do it if he's not comin' back, but that I don't know for sure."

Todd asked, "How long ago did he head to the airport?"

"Just a couple hours ago."

Wow. Todd stepped back and hid his satisfaction upon hearing that. And Mollie said,

"Don't ask me what plane he's on or what time it takes off—or heads where, for that matter—'cause I surely don't know."

"All right. Thank you kindly, ma'am."

He raised his hand as if doffing a hat, even though he wasn't wearing one. Then he pivoted and stepped down off the porch, careful that he didn't step on a rotted plank. Since he didn't have the slightest idea what flight Ralphie might be on or even if it may have already departed, he hurriedly got into his rental car, which already had his luggage in its trunk, and hustled to make the forty-five-minute drive to Pittsburgh International Airport. a massive, crowded and bustling terminal, so much so that how in the hell was he going to find Ralphie Ingram in order to kill him? Common sense told Todd that Ralphie had to be disposed of before he could relax on his own trip without worrying about leaving too many loose ends.

As he drove, he got nervous almost to the point of panic when he contemplated the daunting task of finding Ralphie by checking out dozens and dozens of departure areas. Such a crazy thing might take months instead of minutes. But by the time he ditched the rental car, he knew what he was going to do.

He walked as briskly as he could through the wide front doors of the airport and straight to the Delta Airlines desk. Then, using all the businesslike charm he could muster, he asked one of the boarding clerks, a desirable young black woman in a spiffy uniform, to please make an announcement to help him find his cousin, who had health problems and shouldn't be wandering around on his own.

"Where do you want to meet him, sir?" the clerk asked.

Todd said, "I guess right here. I suppose that'd work best, given the circumstances."

"What do you want me to say?"

Todd told her and in a little while she made the announcement he wanted:

Mr. Ralph Ingram...Mr. Ralph Ingram...Please come to the Delta Airlines Main Desk..."

"I'll get out of the way of your other customers," Todd said. "I may have to use the restroom. But other than that I'll hang around in this area ."After a wait of about twenty minutes, which seemed much longer to Todd, he saw Ralphie coming toward him, looking nervous and wearing ill-fitting, unmatched slacks and a corduroy jacket instead of the bibbed coveralls and clodhoppers Toddy was used to seeing him in.

When Ralphie spotted Tood, he almost jumped out of his skin. As he was backing away, as if to run, Todd seized his elbow and said, "Wait! I'm not here to do you harm. I'm here to give you some money."

"M-money?" Ralphie murmured.

"You did my pals such a big favor they thought they didn't pay you enough, so they sent me to give you more."

"What for?" Ralphie asked shakily.

"For the information you gave them. Don't try to tell me you didn't. I know all about it, Ralphie. You snitched on them and got your palm greased, Didn't you?"

"I ain't sayin' I did and I ain't sayin' I didn't, in case you're wearin' a wire."

Todd thought Ralphie was trying to sound sly and not pulling it off. He said, "C'mon, Ralphie. You want more money, don't you? I think you deserve more."

"How much?" Ralphie said, warming to the idea.

"Two grand," Todd said, smiling engagingly. "For your trip. I didn't extract anything for myself. It's all yours. But I don't want to hand over a bunch of cash right here in the open. Let's do it over there in the men's room."

Todd led the way, and Ralphie followed

In a short while, Ralphie ended up in a commode stall with his throat slit, all his money gone and his body undiscovered for about two hours due to the fact that after exiting the stall, even thoughTodd had no way of locking it, he made sure that Ralphie's shoes and the bottoms of his trousers were showing under the door as if he was sitting on the throne.

CHAPTER 23

Roland and Jocko brought two absolutely stunning young women to Vito and Donna's cookout. They were both tall, tan, and lovely, like the song, "The Girl from Ipanema." At first I thought they were even younger than they were, but as I looked them over I decided that they were both in their thirties, not twenties. They were wearing short skirts, diaphanous blouses, and gold earrings, necklaces and pendants that could have come from Rodeo Drive. I didn't peg them as actresses or models, but instead as highly paid escorts. I didn't begrudge Roland or Jocko if that's how they wanted to spend the money they made by salvaging Spanish galleons or whatever else they might be doing that was less romantic or legal. After all, Roland had to forgo a normal family life during all those years that he was on the run, so he had probably found another way to satisfy his male urges. And so had Jocko.

The young or not-quite-so-young women were introduced to us as Becky and Marie. I immediately forgot their last names but not their looks. Becky was a brunette and Marie was a strawberry-blonde, both spectacularly beautiful from head to toe. The blonde seemed to mostly be attached to Roland, and the other to Jocko. Vito urged the new arrivals to make themselves comfortable and help themselves to snacks and drinks from the bar. I always admired his hosting style, which consisted of good-naturedly encouraging all guests to fend for themselves. In lieu of having to wait on everybody hand and foot, he would say. "My casa is your casa so help yourself to anything you see, and if you want anything that you don't see, just ask me and I'll get it for you if I have it, but if I don't have it, you'll have to make do." He and Donna lived in a modern ranch-style home with an expansive yard and an in-ground swimming pool with six feet of flagstones all around it to keep grass cuttings from going into the water and being a pain in the butt to skim out. The patio was paved with flagstones that matched the ones around the pool and had a roof that created shade depending on where the sun was.

Vito, Donna, my wife Diane, my daughter Joy, her husband Michael, and I were all wearing T-shirts and jeans, some cutoff and some not. Roland was wearing a dark-blue short-sleeved summer shirt and sharply creased white trousers, and Jocko was wearing a black shirt, and tan trousers, and they both wore white loafers that probably cost around three hundred bucks a pair. After a quick glance at each other, they took off their Rolexes and shed all of their clothes except the bathing suits they wore underneath and shouted boisterously as they jumped into the pool, making two huge splashes. We all laughed, including the two lovely female newcomers, who smiled and shook their heads as if to say boys will be boys.

Roland and Jocko started splashing and rough-housing with one another and yelling for the rest of us to jump in, but the women said they didn't want to get their hair wet, including Joy, who normally didn't care about that because even though she was bright and sophisticated in many ways, she was still somewhat of a tomboy—and she proved it by changing her mind about getting her hair wet and jumping into the pool, then zestfully splashing Roland and Jocko till they grabbed her and ducked her and she came up spluttering. By that time I had taken my shirt off and dove in with my pants on because I didn't bring a swimsuit.

When we got tired out from frolicking, we came out of the water and Diane tossed towels at us and we started drying ourselves with the towels, then gave up and let the sun and the summer air finish the job. We helped ourselves to more drinks

110

and snacks while Roland put steaks and corn on the cop on his Grillmaster. And when the food was ready we assembled around a huge redwood picnic table and raved about everything we were eating.

Michael looked like he wasn't having as much fun as the rest of us were, and I noticed his eyes kept fastening upon Becky and Marie, though he tried not to show it. But Joy picked up on her husband's wandering eye anyway and looked annoyed by the whole scene. By the same token, I had noticed him casting nasty looks when Joy was horsing around with Roland and Jocko in the pool.

Michael drank a lot while eating, and by the time he was done he found it harder to pretend he wasn't angry with Joy. He got to his feet almost drunkenly and announced he was going to leave and immediately headed for his car, and Joy went after him. I could hear them arguing in the driveway but couldn't make out what they were saying. And when Joy rejoined us she seemed glum. But in a little while she brightened up. "Michael's being a jerk," she said, "but he's not going to spoil my whole day."

"You just stay put, honey," Diane said. "Donna and I will be the clean-up detail. I really don't mind 'cause we can talk girl talk."

"I want to help too," Becky said, and she started helping Diane and Donna gather up plates and silverware and followed them into the kitchen.

"Wanna play cards?" Roland asked. "Marie's a professional card shark. She can show us all a few tricks."

"Not enough to get over on Becky," Marie said jovially. "She's a dealer at the Three Rivers Casino."

When the picnic table was cleared off enough, Vito went in the house and came back out with trays of poker chips and Marie produced a deck of cards from her purse and started dealing hands of draw poker to me, Joy, Vito, Roland, and Jocko. We played eight or ten hands which resulted in the rest of us having not too many chips left and Marie having a pile of them in front of her. Then she confessed she had been cheating all along and none of us had caught her.

And when she explained in detail why everything had gone her way, I didn't totally catch on and don't remember what she said about it because Diane and Donna rejoined us after cleaning up and putting things away.

We were all getting sleepy, at least I was, but we talked amiably for a while about this and that, but intentionally refrained from mentioning the case we were pursuing. The picnic wrapped up not long after dark and Roland and Jocko and their two girlfriends thanked the host and hostess and said appreciative things to the rest of us, then Roland apologized for leaving, saying his usual, "Got people to see and places to go."

After they drove off in Roland's car, I ventured to say, "I have a suspicion that Becky and Marie are escorts on top of whatever they do at the casino."

"No shit," said Vito. "I knew that from the jump."

"I suspected it," said Joy, and I was alarmed at how streetwise she was becoming.

Donna said, "Well, if that's true, I had no idea. Did you, Diane?"

"No, because my mind's not in the gutter."

"Neither is mine," I countered. "But I can't help taking notice of such things because of all my years working in Hollywood with all its shams and scams."

After a long pause in the conversation, Diane said, "There's something Marie said that made me wonder."

"Like what?" Joy perked up and asked.

"She asked me how far Little Washington was from here. She said one night Jocko was half bagged—those were her words—and when he fell into bed beside her in their motel room, he muttered that he and Roland had a bad run-in with some outlaws down there."

"Aha, the plot thickens," Vito said, jokingly trying to sound like Sherlock Holmes.

I didn't say, "Precisely, Dr. Watson." But that's when it seemed we all felt it was sort of confirmed that Roland and Jocko had probably done some unsavory things behind our back.

CHAPTER 24

Once he arrived in Oklahoma City, Todd Nalepka made a habit of eating and drinking at a saloon not far from the Alfred P. Murrah Federal Building because he wanted to be accepted as a familiar face, a regular customer, not someone to be feared or distrusted. From his online research he had ascertained that this particular joint, The Lonesome Dove—no doubt named after the novel and the TV series of that title—was the habitual hangout of his mark, US Marshall Ryan Burke. He was never wearing his uniform when he came in there; he was always in a suit and tie, even though the suit looked like it came straight off the rack. Todd assumed that the wearing of a uniform was mainly required during times when marshals were in court.

An easy hack into Ryan Burke's job records and bank and mortgage accounts had revealed an array of facts that made him a likely candidate for bribery. At age thirty-nine and married for ten years, all of his credit cards were maxed out or over their limits. His checking account was seven hundred dollars in the red, and he was four months behind in his mortgage. All of that pressure must've been what had led to heavy drinking on Burke's part. Todd had watched him stagger out of The Lonesome Dove three evenings in a row, barely able to walk without bumping into something or falling down. Thus it was clear he was in dire need of the heavy infusion of cash Todd could provide. It would have been nice if Ryan's dire cash needs would have been made even worse by a drug or gambling addiction, but Todd had not learned anything of that sort. But even so, the mark seemed vulnerable enough to warrant a subtle, seemingly casual approach, and if things got too dicey, Todd could back off rather than arouse too much suspicion, then skedaddle onto a flight to somewhere else.

After a week of establishing himself as a regular, Todd took the step of barging into the place in manufactured high spirits, loudly laughing, and boasting of a big hit on a lottery ticket. Right away, some of the patrons congratulated him and shook his hand and tried to pry out of him how much he had won.

"I don't want to brag," he told them all. "Let's just say it was north of thirty grand. Drink up, everybody! It's on me!"

Putting two hundred-dollar bills on the bar he yelled, "I mean it! Make these C-notes disappear!"

Todd was wearing a cheaper suit than he usually wore in order to put himself and Ryan Burke on the same level. Out of the corner of his eye he took note that Ryan, sitting three stools away, was taking advantage of the first round of free drinks. Then another. And another. Then Burke raised his shot glass in a toast to Todd and tossed the shot down after sitting next to him on a stool freshly vacated.

Things seemed to be moving even faster than Todd had hoped, so he turned toward Ryan and said, "Pardon me, sir, but I've noticed you in here before. What brings you in here so often? Are you unmarried? Don't you have a family to go home to?"

Ryan stiffened and pushed back on his stool, giving Todd a hard look.

Todd thought Ryan might take a swing at him if he didn't back off a bit, so he said, "Don't worry, I'm not hitting on you. I'm not gay, not one bit I promise. I guess my curiosity got the best of me."

"Too much curiosity could land you in a courtroom," Ryan said. "I'm a US Marshal. The wrong guy for you to fuck with."

"Sorry…sorry…I apologize," Todd said.

Ryan eyed him for a spell longer, then relaxed. "If you had a wife like mine," he said, "you wouldn't want to go home either. We're in deep debt and she blames it all on me, but she's the one with a shopping addiction."

Todd thought, Great, they're *both* addicts. If I offer them a bailout, they'll jump at it. Piece of cake.

"I think we're headed for a divorce," Ryan said, then tossed down his fourth or fifth shot.

"Another round?" Todd offered.

"I wouldn't say no. But I can't buy you one back. Gotta leave what's in front of me for a tip when I lift my ass off of my stool."

Todd saw that Ryan only had three or four bucks and some change on the bar. The guy was hurting for sure.

Worried about making his move too quickly, Todd let this first day's conversation lapse. But two days later he got to sit next to Ryan again and bought several rounds, not for the house, but just for the two of them, as he carefully introduced money talk once again.

"Well, look, Ryan," he began, lowering his voice and trying to sound honest, sincere, and empathetic, "I just hit a big ticket, as you know. And I don't mind sharing my good fortune because I don't really need cash. I have plenty. I'm a real estate developer from back east, and I do very well for myself. I could make you a loan with better terms than you could get from a bank or a finance company."

Ryan eyed him skeptically. "You'd do that for me? And we don't hardly know each other? You can't be serious."

"Oh, I contribute to all kinds of good causes! Nursing homes, hospices, Meals on Wheels, you name it. I don't mind helping an honest citizen who needs it. Of course I would charge some interest, but nowhere near what a shylock would hit you with, believe me."

"What the hell could be in it for you?" Ryan Burke demanded in a much harsher tone.

116

"Again, I must apologize," Todd answered. "If you don't want my help, that is. I didn't mean to be pushy, but I take the Bible literally. The Good Samaritan part in particular."

"You're a hard dude to fathom," Ryan said. And he got off of his stool, straightened his tie and button his coat, and headed for the door, leaving his tip money on the bar.

"My name is Todd Nelson!" Nalepka called after him.

"Ryan Burke," Ryan turned halfway around and mumbled.

The next time that the two men drank together, with Todd paying for every round, after Ryan was loosened up quite a bit, Todd said, "Since you're a US Marshal, I assume you work at that building that's so notorious. Stop me if I'm saying something I shouldn't, but did you happen to be there when it was bombed?"

"Aw, man, I really hate to talk about that," Ryan said, running his hand over his brow and through his hair, which was already mussed up and sweaty from alcohol.

But Ryan didn't seem to get mad so Todd said, "I imagine a fellow like you would've saved a lot of lives that day. You're probably in real hero. Which is another reason I wouldn't mind helping you out financially."

Ryan answered slowly, thoughtfully, and hesitantly. "Well...I've actually been thinking about that...and I guess I'd be pretty stupid if I put you off out of stubbornness or a misplaced sense of pride or something."

"Let me help you. There's no shame in that," Todd said as kindly as he could. "I'll give you cash out of my lottery winnings. We'll do it on a handshake, nothing needs to be written down so you don't have to worry about repercussions. Just a handshake between two men as good as their word. Like John Wayne. Or the way Dean Martin did it with his longtime friend and manager."

"I didn't know that," Ryan said with a chuckle. "Where would the cash change hands do you think?"

117

"My motel room would be a good place. I'm staying at the Rodeo Inn, room 119."

"I'm gonna be really busy the next two nights," Ryan said. "Can we do it on Friday?"

This rang an alarm bell in Todd's mind because it wasn't like a man in severe need of money to put the acquisition of it off for a couple of days. But nevertheless he said, "Certainly, we can pick a time."

But when Todd was lying on one of the twin beds in room 119 that night, lots of things were going through his mind. He remembered all that had transpired between him and Ryan Burke by rote and replayed it over and over.

It had all the earmarks of a sting.

In other words, he was being played all along even as he believed he was the player and Ryan was the mark.

Todd believed that all of his research and prying that showed Ryan was in dire financial circumstances was accurate and not to be faulted. But now it seemed that in spite of those kinds of problems Ryan was a tried and true United States Marshal, totally committed and not to ready to betray his oath.

The "two days" was the clue.

Todd realized that it was highly likely that the delay would give the lawmen time to bug the very room he was in, lying on one of the beds. It would be rigged with both video and audio to capture the money changing hands. And the sting would land Todd in jail.

He was impelled to stare raging and cursing, but he didn't dare. And the futility enraged him even more.

He decided to clear out in the morning. Just pack up and head out and grab another flight, all his work wasted in a horrible, hard-to-take way.

He wished he could turn the tables on Ryan Burke first, and for a time he mulled over different ways he might be able to pull it off. But as he tamped down his anger, he became more

118

resigned, more acclimated to the idea that he hadn't fallen prey to the sting and would live to fight another day.

CHAPTER 25

In July of 2003 Vito, Joy, and I were trying to figure out our next move and weren't very happy with ourselves for not being able to get Roland Fornier's granddaughter and great-granddaughter back for him. Nothing had opened up for us. We were stumped. We didn't know what names she and her daughter were using when they were put into Witness Protection or what names they were using these days. So how the hell were we supposed to put a trace on them?

However, Joy came up with an idea for a random kind of search that sounded like a shot in the dark to me, because I'm "technologically challenged." In the midst of our glumness over our lack of success, she perked up just a bit, her blue eyes lighting up a little, and said, "Let's try Facebook."

"Facebook,"?" I said dismissively, wondering how she could actually suggest such a thing. "They could be having a ball on there under their new identities and we wouldn't even know how to *friend* them."

"I'm surprised you know that, term, Dad," Joy said, joshing me.

Celebrity that I am, I do maintain a Facebook fan page for promotional purposes—but I'm notorious for not keeping up with it. And I shun all other social media sites because it bugs me that they exist. Sometimes I want to toss my computer out the window, even though it makes word processing, which used to be called "writing," so much easier. Maybe I should've been born a couple centuries ago.

Joy said, "Lots of missing people like teenage runaways and even murder victims, have been found or identified by friends and relatives by posting about them on social media. In some instances they've actually solved mysteries that the cops couldn't."

"Vito could've tried that on his own," I said. "He wouldn't have needed us."

"He's probably as Internet challenged as you are, DadVito jumped in and said, "Believe it or not, I think it's worth a try. How would we go about it, Joy?"

"Well, if we set up a site for her, we could ask her to please get in touch with us. We could post photos of Katherine and Magda from around the time of the trial, but maybe photoshopped a little, at least on Katherine, but nothing drastic. I don't think we should come out and say who she is, or was, either, because that might draw the wrong kind of attention to her or might totally scare her off, because she's gotta still be scared of Kirk Biggins's former associates." Vito pursed his lips, a sober, contemplative look on his face. He said, "Before we do any of this we've got to get approval from Roland Fornier. Why don't we see if we can get him on speakerphone so we can make our case and gauge his reaction?'

"I've got him in my contact list. I'll make the call," Joy said. "Then I'll tie you guys in."

Luckily she got Roland on the line, told him that the three of us wanted to talk with him about something important, and after Vito and I were conferenced in, she laid out the plan we had been considering.

Roland listened without comment, then said, "You're not gonna mention me, are you—because that'll give the game away."

"No, that's for sure," Vito said. "We've already banished any thought of that."

Joy said, "I can create a site that just asks Katherine, whatever she's going by now, to get in touch with her grandfather. I have a second thought concerning her daughter, too. I think we should leave her out of it. Even if a few things were done to alter her appearance, she's probably still more recognizable in her present state that her mother is. And plus, the mother-child combination would be too revealing."

"Damn! Joy is one smart cookie," Roland said over the speaker phone.

"Thanks," Joy answered.

I said, "Then we have your tentative approval, Roland? Till you see the proposed website that Joy will create?" "Yeah, let's at least go that far, for now," he answered.

After we all got off of the phone call, Vito said, "I think this is a good idea—in fact, the most viable idea we really have. We're asking her to come to us rather than the other way around. At least it has a chance. But let's give it some more thought to see if we can shoot any holes in it. I mean the kind of holes that can put the grandchild and *her* child in more danger than they might already be in."

Joy stood up from the conference table and said, apologetically, "Is it okay if I take off? I can work on a prototype for a Facebook announcement at home and figure out which other outlets might be useful. But my husband and I have plans that I shouldn't cancel."

"Fine with me," Vito said. "See you in the morning. I'll be anxious to see what you come up with."

"Me too, honey," I told her.

She put on a light denim jacket, gathered up her purse and her laptop, and told us goodbye. As soon as she was gone Vito said, "Let's go to The Interchange for a drink and a sandwich, if you're up for it, Dave. We can both go in my car and I'll drop you off back here when we leave."

Nothing much was said in the car except some light banter about how the Pittsburgh Pirates were doing—last place as usual. They had won several World Series over the years but that kind of season had existed only in the past for a couple of decades. But once we were seated on bar stools in a corner where there weren't other patrons too close to us, our conversation turned toward aspects of Roland Fornier's case, especially the prospects of hitting on something important due to Joy's idea of using the Internet. Both of us admitted she was the young expert in such matters and we were the old fogies, but we also expressed our hopes that she would somehow pull on the right string.

Our beers came and we sipped. Then Vito asked me, "Did Joy tell you why she's going somewhere with Michael this evening?"

I admitted that she hadn't.

"They're going to a counseling session," Vito said. "For some time now I've had the feeling that their marriage might be on the rocks, so I finally made so bold a move as to ask her about it one day at the office. Maybe I shouldn't have…because it made her cry. She tried to hold back tears but she didn't succeed. I felt like hell for opening my big mouth, so I apologized, but she said she was actually glad I asked because she needed to confide in somebody and she felt funny about using you as a confessor because you're her dad."

The news actually didn't hit me as hard as Vito might've thought, because just like him, I had picked up on some bad vibes between my son-in-law and my daughter even though they had tried to hide them.

"Does your wife know? Or my wife?" I asked him.

"Donna doesn't, but I don't know about Diane."

Even though Diane was my second wife and not Joy's biological mother, Joy and Diane had always been close. But I felt pretty sure that if Joy had confided in her, she wouldn't have kept it from me.

"I'm going to keep my distance," I said to Vito. "I'm not going to horn in unless I'm asked. "Maybe the counseling sessions will work. Not that I have a great deal of confidence in such things. But they need space to solve their own problems. They don't need me muddling things up."

"That's what I hoped you'd say," Vito told me. "Should we order sandwiches or something? The steak hoagies are great."

"I know," I said. "And if I order the whole thing with french fries and coleslaw, instead of the half hoagie, I can bring some dinner home for my wife."

CHAPTER 26

Joy's prototype web page, not launched yet but created so we could troubleshoot it, had as its banner a photo montage composed of three images of Katherine. One was from television coverage of her trial and the other two were photoshopped images versions of how she may have changed her looks.

The copy said: "This young mother may be in danger, and we want to protect her! She left the Witness Protection Program recently and we don't know how she looks now, what name she may be using, or where she might be living and working. We can't reveal her birth name because it may compromise her safety and that of her child. If you think you may know her or have information about her, no matter how tenuous, please contact us by filling in the form on this site. Your name will not be revealed."

Once again, Vito, Joy, and I were in the conference room in Vito's office, and this time we were looking at what Joy had created, trying to troubleshoot it, and wondering if it was going to bring more trouble down on us or Roland Fornier's daughter than we could handle. Vito looked up at us and said to Joy, "Did you send this to Roland yet?"

She said, "Yes, but I phoned him first and delicately explained what was coming to him and that it wouldn't be launched without his approval."

"Well, now that I see it in front of me, I don't think it has a snowball's chance in hell of actually working," Vito said.

I said, "I have severe doubts, too. Not to criticize you or what you've done, here, Joy, but I'm really afraid we're going to get a lot of phony tips and crank calls and even worse, if anybody is out to kidnap or murder Katherine, we'll be firing them up all the more."

But right then, before we had any chance to beat it around some more, my cell phone chimed and Roland was on the line.

He said, "I looked over this thing that Joy sent me, and I want to speak my piece. If Vito and Joy are with you, put me on speaker phone."

I did so, and Roland surprised us by saying, "I think Joy basically has a good idea, but it's not strong enough to flush Katherine out. I think we have to be bolder even if it means taking a much bigger chance."

"You mean putting her in danger?" I felt impelled to ask.

"Hopefully not," said Roland. "But I think we have to say that I love her and I want to welcome her back—something like that anyway—or else we're gonna get nowhere fast. Joy is right in thinking that if we don't have a clue as to where she is, we have to somehow draw her to *us*. This thing does attempt to do that, but it's too weak. In for a penny, in for a pound, so to speak. We can't tiptoe around this thing at this point because we might have enemies we don't even know about and if so, they're not gonna keep their powder dry like we are."

"You have a point, Roland," Vito said. "But how're you gonna feel if we get her and her daughter killed?"

There was a long pause. Then Roland said, "Make me another draft, Joy. And make it stronger and more to the point. Then we can either tweak it and put it out, or delete it from your files and never talk about it again. But keep in mind that we'd have to come up with something that has a chance of working without causing harm. We'd have to track Katherine down using old-fashioned methods that don't seem to apply in this situation."

Joy took a deep breath and said, "Let me clarify, Roland. You want me to put your actual name out in hopes that Katherine will see it and get in touch. Or else somebody who knows her as she is now will get in touch even if she doesn't."

"That's right," said Roland.

And Joy said, "All right I'll give it a shot. I'll do up a stronger probe and we'll run it by you for your approval."

"Makes sense to me," Roland said. "So get started. Jocko and I are still down here in Fort Lauderdale but I'm gonna rent a house up your way. That way we can work more closely together, in person. I made already paid two months' worth of rent and signed the lease, so I can give you an address in case it needs to be on the web site Joy is gonna set up. But don't launch it till I give the go ahead."

"We already made that promise," Vito said.

"Yeah, I know, I know," said Roland. "I'm just making sure."

After we ended the conference call, Joy said to me, "Your friend's kind of abrupt, isn't he?"

"He can be," I said. "When he's in his man-of-action mode he's a man of few words. But other times he and Jocko can wax poetic—or wax doggerel, if there is such a thing. Back in the late fifties or early sixties, I think, there was a TV Western series starring Richard Boone as an erudite gunslinger named Paladin who spouted Shakespeare and handed out business cards that said *Have Gun, will Travel.*"

"In other words, a hitman," Joy pointed out, interrupting me. "Maybe one of their early role models if the rumors are true."

"Could be," I conceded after thinking about it in that way for the first time. "Roland and Jocko fell in love with the Paladin mystique and tried to talk and act just like him, as if their own lives as loose cannons and bar room bawlers were somehow cut from the same cloth. They used a lot of words like hark and hath and be gone infidel like they heard Richard Boone use but they didn't use them artfully. One time I was drinking with them at a bar in Clairton and a barfly tried to sucker punch Roland, but

Roland stopped the guy's fist in midair and judo-chopped him to the floor. The guy laid there for a while, then he pulled himself halfway up by the rungs of Roland's bar stool and grabbed hold of Roland's testicles. *Hark, Jocko, he hath me by the balls!* Roland cried out, then he chopped the guy down again, grabbed him by the seat of his pants and the scruff of his neck, bum-rushed him into the alley and stuffed him into a garbage can!" "I heard about that at the time," Vito said, chuckling. "I was wishing I was there to see it. I thought it was pretty cool back then."

"Me too," I said. "I used to tell people about it when I was stoned."

"Dad!" Joy said, shooting me a startled glance.

"What?" I said. "You think I wasn't a creature of the fifties and sixties?"

"Back then I'd have arrested you if I caught you," Vito said. "Later I started smoking weed too. But I had to hide it more than you did since I was a cop."

"What about you, Joy? Fess up," I said.

"I'm not going to tell on myself," she said staunchly.

"Well, never mind," said Vito. "We can guess what the answer would be if you weren't trying so hard to be coy."

"I'm outta here," she said. "Michael will be waiting for me and he gets mad if I'm late."

She hurriedly grabbed her stuff.

"I thought he was your husband, not your boss." I couldn't help saying it, then silently berated myself for not keeping my mouth shut.

But Joy let it pass. She just pivoted and walked out.

Not long after, I wondered when a parent should stop worrying about a son or a daughter and concluded that there was no end to it. We're totally invested in them from the time they're conceived until the day we die. I suspected that Joy had to meet Michael because they were going to one of their marriage counseling sessions, and I could only hope they were going well. The counselor that Joy and Michael had been seeing was a minister of the Unitarian persuasion, which in my opinion was where people ended up when they didn't very much believe in Christianity any longer but didn't want to admit that they didn't go to church.

I was what some people would call "a fallen Catholic" but I believed that I had risen above the indoctrination. Nevertheless I could concede that maybe the church's rigid moral strictures and emphasis on sin had grounded me in my youth, so that I could mature toward intellectual freedom as I grew older without becoming a nihilist or something worse.

Joy was only three when my first wife and I got divorced with joint custody, and with the need to care for my child's physical and intellectual development partly in my hands, I was forced to consider if I should raise her like I was raised, in other words under the "firm guidance" of a religion, thereby giving her some solid, if erroneous, beliefs to stand on, before maturing away from any them as an awareness of shades of gray slowly took over—almost like a dawning awareness that there really isn't a Santa Claus.

My ex-wife and I talked it over fairly intensely on a number of occasions, and she opted to at least take Joy to Sunday school now and then, even though she wasn't much more religious than I was. By age six or seven Joy began to wonder why the parents of her friends and classmates were church-goers and I wasn't. But I didn't try to make her into a nonbeliever. Instead I took her to any church she wanted to go to from time to time, and I went with her without putting any of them down. All the way into her high school years, we "worshipped" with an intermittent succession of congregations including Catholics, Methodists, Presbyterians, Jews, Quakers, Unitarians, and what have you, and ultimately her curiosity was satisfied and she did not become a member of any of them.

So it came to pass that when she and her husband decided to try marriage counseling, Joy wanted to go to a secular psychologist while Michael, whose Lutheran upbringing came to the forefront now that his relationship with Joy was in trouble, insisted that they should consult with a clergyman. Joy was repelled by that idea and did not give in so easily, but eventually they compromised by choosing a Unitarian minister.

Joy told me all this, alternately laughing and crying, after she abandoned therapy in favor of a separation that was destined to become final. In fact it all went to pieces on the same day she headed out of Vito's office saying that she had to meet Michael or he'd get angry. She sat still for that day's counseling session, which was number eight or nine by her reckoning, then when they got home, she told Michael she wasn't gonna go to any more of them. "I feel like a child being scolded," she told him. "That minister can't hide the fact that he's on your side."

Neither of them filed for a divorce the next day, or for weeks afterward, but eventually that's what it came to.

I liked Michael and wished him well and even hoped that he and I could somehow remain friends. I couldn't help thinking that perhaps if I had found it in me to champion his screenplay, even though I didn't fully believe in it, he and my daughter might still be together. I was thankful Joy didn't seem to be blaming me in any way. When push came to shove, I knew she was a strong, independent young woman as resilient as any of the female characters in my movies. Which didn't mean that she wasn't suffering quite a bit after the breakup, and my heart ached for her.

CHAPTER 27

For over three hours on top of the man hours spent on previous days, Todd Nalepka had been surfing the technological world of the huge wide-screen computer in his master bedroom.

For over three hours he had been plugging in keywords as fast as he could make them up. Then he suddenly felt the pure joy of a stunning discovery. It was a newly launched web page dedicated to a search for just one person whose varying images on the site's banner bore a resemblance to Katherine Biggins as he remembered her from televised coverage of her trial. He hunched forward, tingling with excitement, his whitened knuckles clenching the armrests of his high and wide black-leather executive chair, and read the announcement several times over:

This young mother may be in danger! She left the Witness Protection Program and did not disclose where she was going. She may not exactly resemble the likenesses of her that you see here. We want her to know that her grandfather still loves her and wants to protect her. If you think you may know her, please contact us at: VICTOR MARTIN ASSOCIATES.

There was a 1-800 number and an email address, but of course Todd Nalepka had no intention of using them. With the brand new direction he could go in now, he told himself he could soon put the bitter disappointment of Oklahoma City behind him. The memory of almost falling prey to a sting still rankled his bruised ego, even in the glow of this beckoning discovery. With a gloating smile on his face, he pictured himself capturing the erstwhile Katherine Biggins and keeping her prisoner in the windowless steel container on the hundred acres of property he owned, not far from his condo. None of his other victims had been found there, nor did he think Katherine would be found inside his homemade cell before he made use of her and then got rid of her like all the others.

His first step toward that pleasantly enticing goal was to do a detailed Web search on the grandfather mentioned in the online posting. He readily remembered the man's name from back when he was watching the trial. Roland Fornier. He was the key to Katherine. That was an absolute.

He soon found that Fornier was a treasure hunter who had become enormously wealthy by investing in a seagoing outfit that had salvaged a Spanish galleon. Todd found articles and photos galore on that amazing event that transpired in Fort Lauderdale. Roland Fornier was described as a modern-day soldier of fortune.

Todd Napeka smirked to himself thinking Roland's fortunes were about to take a tumble if he indeed turned out to be successful in luring his granddaughter to him along with her six-year-old child. Ransom was a fine augmentation to capture and torture. Maybe he should start calling himself RCT, like that dumbass who had gotten caught after sending boastful notes to the Kansas City newspapers signed "BTK"—Burn, Torture, Kill.

Todd began dreaming of how he could use a huge ransom paid from the gold and silver of a Spanish galleon to make the Aryan Confederacy rise from its ashes with himself as leader and in control of plenty enough money to rebuild a heavily armed militia and explode enough dirty bombs to bring the Zionist Occupational Government, in fact the entire United States of American, to its knees.

CHAPTER 28

I could barely sleep at night because I was on pins and needles worrying that Roland's amended version of Joy's Internet announcement wouldn't work and scared that it actually would. In suggesting the revisions, in fact vigorously insisting on them, Roland had said on the speakerphone, "Listen, you guys. We don't have the vaguest idea how to get to Katherine, so the next best thing is to draw her to us."

"That's what I'm afraid of," Vito had said. "We'd be taking one hell of a chance. It could be that she'd make her way here with a pack of vicious sons of bitches trailing after her."

Roland's answer to that was, "Jocko and I can handle the motherfuckers. Sorry, Joy, I forgot to rein in my toilet tongue. I apologize for that."

"But you're using your daughter and her toddler for bait," Joy scolded him. "Frankly I don't like it."

"It's not much different from the cops convincing witnesses to wear wires to get the goods on murderers. I'll bet Vito didn't blanche at that tactic. That's the kind of cop he used to be."

"You have a point," Vito acknowledged, casting a look at Joy as if wondering what she thought of him.

Resigned, she said, "Okay, you make the call, Vito. I'll stop being a naysayer. It's just that I've never willingly put anybody but myself in danger."

This might have been a dig at me and Vito both because on a previous case when we were trying to protect Joy from a sneak attack by a suspected serial killer, we had staked her out without telling her so as not to scare her too much. We didn't have enough evidence to have the suspect detained and we weren't sure what he was going to do. It turned out that while Vito and I were in surveillance mode, staking Joy's house out from concealment, the suspect did make his move and Vito shot and killed him. I always believed, probably because I really wanted to, that Joy understood and forgave what we did. But maybe she had lingering doubts.

"I'm sure we all empathize with whatever concerns Joy has," Roland said over the speakerphone. "But dangerous times require dangerous counter measures. I'm giving you my approval to put the Internet thing in action with the revisions I'll email to you. Jocko and I are moving into the house not far from you in a week or so. That's where we'll direct Katherine to, should we be lucky enough to hear from her."

"I'll be hoping we don't suffer any unintended consequences," Joy said with a touch of irony.

Roland let it pass, said his goodbyes and good lucks to us, and ended the conference call.

There was a long period of uneasy silence, then Vito said, "I'm worried that Roland is itching for consequences that are more intended than not."

Joy and I both knew what Vito meant. All three of us were suspecting that Roland and Jocko were itching for the bad guys to come right *to* them. If they got the chance, they would take them by surprise and exterminate them like vermin.

"They think they'd be doing the world a favor," Vito said.

"But what can we do about it?" Joy asked. "Just stand by knowing we're watching a planned execution?"

"Maybe that wouldn't need to happen if we could somehow intercept the bad guys first," I mused disconsolately.

"Not us, but maybe the feds," Joy suggested, amending my suggestion.

"We'd play hell to try to get the feds involved," Vito said. "Damn! This case was scary and a tough nut to crack and now it's gotten worse."

Neither Joy nor I had anything to say to that.

CHAPTER 29

Surfing the Internet during her lunch hour, with a pumpkin latte and a bagel spread with strawberry creamed cheese to one side of her computer, Sarah Jamison was trying to find out if anyone was searching for her. For the past six or seven years she had immersed in this routine at least twice each week, with a mixture of wariness, fear, and curiosity. Complete peace of mind would elude her so long as she had to deal with the possibility that the remnants of the Aryan Confederacy would not only never forgive her for killing Kirk Biggins but also would not let go of their certainty that she had stolen his secrets. The curiosity centered around remembrances of her grandfather, Roland Fornier, whom she had come to believe was the only person who had ever truly cared about her in a pure and benevolent way.

She did her searches mainly on sites dedicated to missing persons, and when she moved her mouse across the screen she was simultaneously hopeful and frightened that she would hit on her own face. And when it actually happened that day, she held her slice of bagel in midair.

...her grandfather still loves her...

Those were the words that stuck in her mind. Going back to him had been a recurrent pipedream. But after she saw Internet articles about his participation in the salvage of Spanish treasure, she was scared he would think that greed was her motive for doing so. She didn't want him to think she was like Kirk in any way. She didn't want anything that wasn't hers, but maybe it wouldn't for long be his either because the latest postings about the salvage operation stated that the Spanish government was

136

going to be awarded the bulk of the half-billion dollars in gold and silver. It seemed to Sarah that her grandfather probably wasn't going to be enormously rich after all. But apparently, he wasn't giving up. He had recently posted a ten-minute video with himself as spokesman concerning a new salvage venture called Fornier Treasure Hunters LLC, for which he was seeking investors. That was just like him, she told herself with a smile, to be shameless enough to make himself the star of the glittering and glamorous enterprise, even if some people might think it gauche to put his own name on it.

No way was she going to call attention to herself by calling the 1-800 number on the missing person site. She had no way of knowing if it was legit. It might be a setup designed to lure her and her daughter into the clutches of someone intent on doing them harm.

After considerable deliberation, she Googled the phone number and address of Fornier Treasure Hunters in Fort Lauderdale, Florida, and when a female voice answered, she asked if she could please speak with Roland Fornier.

"He's not here right now," the receptionist said. "To whom may I direct you?"

Sarah was pleased that she wasn't getting immediately brushed off. She told herself it must be because they were in seeking-investors mode and didn't want to turn anybody away that might turn out to be for real.

"I'm a personal friend of Roland's," Sarah said. "I know he's seeking investors but I don't want to speak with anyone except him."

"Well…if you want to leave your name and phone number or email," the receptionist said, "I can make sure he gets the information when he calls in."

"Where is he now?" Sarah dared to ask.

"In Pittsburgh, Pennsylvania. He's in the midst of a relocation. But I can't tell you exactly where without his permission."

"That's okay," said Sarah. "Thank you for your help."

She ended the call and promptly started another online search. Figuring that if her grandfather was relocating, he'd probably be buying a house rather than renting a place, because that was his style, she searched for recent property acquisitions in Pittsburgh and its suburbs. In forty-five minutes or so she had her answers, and she wrote them down. For the rest of her workday, she didn't get her quota of tax returns filled out because she was trying to figure out the best way to utilize what she had learned.

She allowed herself to entertain a glimmer of hope that getting back in touch with her grandfather might open up new vistas for herself and her daughter.

CHAPTER 30

In considering what might be the best way and the most opportune place to kidnap the former Katherine Biggins, the major obstacle for Todd Nalepka was that he had no idea where she *was*. Obviously that was the same obstacle that had been faced by her grandfather, Roland Fornier, and Fornier must have arrived at the conclusion that if he couldn't go to *her*, he must get her to come to *him*. Hence the postings on the Internet.

Assuming that the lure would sooner or later have its desired effect, Todd knew that he would need to figure out how to intercept its target. Since he didn't know where Katherine would start out from, he would need to somehow be lurking in the vicinity of wherever she had to arrive and he had to pounce on her without getting himself caught or killed.

Furthermore, how would she travel? By plane, train, or car? If by plane, her grandfather would surely meet her when she landed at Greater Pittsburgh International Airport, a dangerous and nearly impossible place for Todd to intercept her and make his getaway. If by train? Let's just scratch that, Todd thought, because that choice seemed unlikely to him. He decided she very well might drive if she lived somewhere close, especially since she would almost certainly be bringing little Magda, which most likely would no longer be her name, to meet her grandfather for the first time, and it would be easier to bring her in a car seat than to go through all the hassle of airport security. Plus, the child probably didn't have a passport yet or any other form of personal ID.

It had been easy to find out the address of the new home Roland Fornier had purchased in Baldwin Borough, an upscale community off of Route 51 South, halfway between Clairton and Pittsburgh. Todd had scouted it out three times. It was a lovely brick ranch on a relatively secluded tree-lined avenue where all the homes had sculpted shrubbery and well maintained but not overly expansive lawns, and no two houses looked exactly the same. Roland's home wasn't fenced in but was partly encircled by hedges trimmed too low to offer concealment.

Todd wanted to be ready to pounce when either Roland or Katherine pulled into the driveway with the little girl in whichever car they would use, but considering the layout of the place it seemed too dumb and too risky.

He pondered an idea that was based upon the possibility that Katherine would be coming to Pittsburgh on the Pennsylvania turnpike. If so, he could lie in wait at one of the exits she might take. But which one? Monroeville or Irwin? Probably Monroeville, the nearest one to the home Roland Fornier had purchased. But how would Todd know when? He couldn't just choose one potential exit and stay nearby from now till Doomsday. Every plan he thought about and troubleshot had big holes in it.

So what *would* work? And how soon? Nothing totally realistic came to mind. But he had to quickly come up with something ironclad because Katherine might already be on her way.

Lost in the intricacies of what he needed to do, he kept on casing Roland Fornier's new home, hoping to ascertain exactly when Fornier would be moving in. To carry on with this, he always drove his Cadillac SUV which fit in nicely with the kinds of vehicles mostly seen around the neighborhood.

Then, on one of his drive-bys, the solution to all of his problems came to him when he saw an electrician's van parked in the Omni stone driveway.

He parked a short distance away and furtively got out of his black SUV with a large switchblade knife in his pocket and a 9mm Glock tucked in his belt.

He went up onto the front porch of Fornier's house and found the door unlocked, as would be expected if movers or craftsmen were at work inside. He hoped that the electrician was working alone, and that turned out to be the case. The house was a split-entry, and he smelled fresh paint as he crept down a short flight of carpeted stairs into the family room, where plastic was on the floor to catch drops of yellow paint that was still drying. It was a piece of cake to catch the electrician off guard. He was connecting the wires on a home entertainment system, and as he turned and looked up, Todd rushed him, snicked the switchblade open and slit his throat.

There was a gush of blood, but no scream—because the larynx was slit along with the jugular—and Todd thought how lucky he was that clean-up would be easy because of the plastic painter's tarp that had already been laid down.

He would have to wrap the electrician's body up in the tarp, load it into the cargo bay of his vehicle, take it away, and dump it. But first he would plant four or five listening devices in different parts of the house, hoping they would give him the edge he needed so badly.

CHAPTER 31

I was feeling badly that over a span of six days the Internet posting that Joy had edited to Roland's specifications had been shared everywhere that Joy deemed plausible, without resulting in any contact at all from Roland's granddaughter. In the meantime, Roland's move into his new residence in Baldwin Borough had been made a fait accompli, and in spite of all his worries, he decided to hold a housewarming party on a Tuesday night in the first week of July. I didn't know exactly why he was doing that. But I didn't try to talk him out of it, which would've been futile.

My wife Diane and I arrived early, and Joy was already in the kitchen helping Donna whip up some things at the last minute. She came as a single because she and Michael were moving onward with their divorce, which so far as I could tell was devoid of fireworks, which might not have been the case had there been children in the mix.

Jocko barged through the front door yelling, "I'm here! Where the hell's the party!?" With him were the two young ladies, Becky and Marie, who had been with Roland and Jocko at Vito's cookout, looking like Victoria Secrets specimens. This time they were in evening gowns.

Three additional couples made their appearance before long, middle-aged people dressed conservatively but expensively in suits and dresses of somber colors that were accessorized with costly jewelry. I didn't recognize any of them and hoped I hadn't met them somewhere before, because it was possible that I had. Much to my embarrassment, I'm absolutely horrible with names and faces. When I'm at movie conventions, I have to keep apologizing to my fans and joking lamely that I meet thousands of people each year and if I could remember all their names I could run for office. On top of it, I have a hard time remembering roads and directions, so much so that when GPS devices started being advertised, Diane immediately bought me one for my birthday. She tells people I only married her for her sense of direction.

Roland didn't have that affliction or else he wouldn't have been such a good salesman. He was very good about introducing or reintroducing everyone by name so that no one had to display perfect recall. It turned out that two of the male counterparts and one of the female counterparts of the three newly arrived couples were officers of major corporations that were headquartered in Pittsburgh, so I assumed Roland must be schmoozing them for investment in Fornier Treasure Hunters LLC. They probably pulled down salaries and perks each year that would have financed three of my movies. Not to mention stock options and golden parachutes. Executives of the major motion picture studios were probably in that category, but even though I was both famous and notorious I was not filthy rich.

Tobe Hooper, who directed *The Texas Chainsaw Massacre* on almost zero bucks, then graduated to mega-budgeted movies like *Poltergeist,* once told me very early in my career, that he was a low millionaire, thus disabusing me of the notion that he must be swimming in cash. The millions of dollars pulled in by his movies were siphoned off by distributors with highly paid teams of lawyers and "creative accountants." I learned the hard way that movie distributors don't want to make movies, they just want to distribute them. Whoever touches the money first keeps it. That's why hired guns like me try to get all they can up front. Points on the back end sound good on paper but seldom pay off. After a long, successful career in the biz, my assets were triple what Tobe had claimed his were, but even so I wasn't a tycoon.

143

In spite of Jocko's boisterous personality and Roland's charisma, the housewarming party turned out to be one of those things where people mostly stood around or sat around with drinks in their hands and talked about things that revealed they had little in common. Some of the moribund aspects of the gathering were attributable to the fact that Roland and Jocko huddled with the corporate executives at the well-stocked bar in his large family room much of the time, with their eye-popping young ladies as window dressing, while the rich men tried to ogle them without being obvious about it and the rich women tried not to look miffed. Vito, Donna, Joy, and I were huddled in a grouping of easy chairs at a distance from the bar except when we went there for refills. I didn't fault Roland for carrying on with his schmoozing in spite of our so-far-unsuccessful hunt for his granddaughter and her child. I knew he could hide his emotions when he had to, and that it didn't mean he didn't have any.

At one point he caught me in the hallway between the powder room and the living room and said in a hushed voice, "Why do you think we haven't heard anything?"

"I wish I knew," I murmured. "Nothing on your end either?"

He said, "Fuck no." Then he pivoted and rejoined his moneyed friends.

I wish we had known at the time that his granddaughter was trying to get to him even as we were pantomiming peace and serenity at the housewarming party. We wouldn't have been able to pull it off if we had known that Todd Nalepka, an evil sonofabitch that we had never heard of, was listening to everything that was going on at Roland's house.

CHAPTER 32

Roland phoned me at half-past three the day after the housewarming party. He sounded like something had occurred that he wanted to be happy about that he couldn't allow himself to celebrate too soon. As if making a police report, he said, "Dave, I finally heard from Katherine and she's driving the turnpike on her way here with little Magda. They're calling themselves Sarah and Laura Jamison now. According to Sarah—I have to get used to that—she should be here by six this evening. Stand by, pal. I'll let you know soon as she arrives."

"Should I let Vito and Joy know?" I asked him warily.

"Let's hold off on that till I see her face-to-face and feel her out some."

But six p.m. came and went and I got no follow-up call. I started to worry but told myself that Roland's reunion with his daughter and granddaughter was probably requiring more adjustment between the three of them. There must have been kinks that needed to be ironed out before it would be wise to bring more people into the mix as a welcoming committee.

It was past seven when Roland finally called me back. He said disconsolately, "She never got here. I don't know what I'm supposed to make of it."

"Maybe a breakdown on the turnpike?"

"Too much of a coincidence. I have a feeling something has happened to her. I don't think she's changed her mind and turned around to drive back to wherever she was coming from. I think this could be bad."

"What exit was she supposed to take?"

"Irwin. I told her she could get here quicker by taking Route 30, not by getting off in Monroeville."

"Should we alert the police? Did she tell you what kind of car she's driving?"

"No, I didn't think it mattered. But now I could kick myself in the ass."

"I offered to meet her at a gas station in Irwin so she could follow me the rest of the way, but she sounded uncomfortable with that. Under the circumstances, I asked her if she thought she might be being followed by somebody and she said no."

"Where's Jocko?" I asked. "In case you need him."

"He and his good-looking wench flew back to Florida."

We talked some more but didn't know what else we could do except and wait and hope that there was some ordinary reason for Katherine/Sarah to have been delayed and that she would soon show up.

CHAPTER 33

After taking the Irwin exit, paying the turnpike toll, and taking the long, curving ramp onto Route 30, Sarah Jamison got an uneasy feeling that she was being followed by a black SUV. To test whether her trepidation was real or unreal, she made a right turn on a two-lane road leading into the small town of Irwin, then several more turns—and to her dismay the black SUV stayed with her, seeming to purposely hang back like a cat waiting for a mouse to come out of its hole.

She passed the Irwin police station and thought of pulling her white Pontiac 6000 over to the curb, with no intention of getting Laura out of her booster seat and going in, but just to scare the driver of the black SUV off. But she didn't enter the police station at all. Instead she kept going for another two blocks then hung a left turn onto a side street and she was relieved when the vehicle that she thought was tracking her did not make that same left turn but shot right past it, and she caught a glimpse of it doing so in her rearview mirror.

She made a hasty right at the next block, then a left, which put her on her way back to Route 30.

Damn it! There was that black SUV again, pulling out from a gas station lot, as if its driver had already known what she would have to do to resume heading for her grandfather's house. She couldn't make out much more than a shadowy image of the driver due to the fact that the SUV had tinted windows, which were illegal in Pennsylvania.

She wished she had a gun, but she hadn't dared to face a background check under the name Sarah Jamison. She had thought of going out and acquiring one in one of the high-crime and dope-infested sections of Philadelphia, but she was scared of getting arrested in some kind of a sting or getting pulled over in possession of an illegal firearm. But just having one would have bolstered her ability to protect her daughter and herself. She was proficient with different types of handguns, thanks to target shooting with her Kirk Biggins, who might still be alive if he hadn't coached her so well.

The black SUV made the same turn she did onto Route 30. She now had little doubt that its driver must be intending her harm. And she had no idea who, or why.

Could it be that somebody had found out that she was going to try to mend the fences between herself and her grandfather? So far as she knew, he was the only one who was wise to where she was going and what route she would take. Could it be that he had actually hired somebody to intercept her, then stick with her and protect her? But somehow, she didn't believe that. She believed that she and her daughter were in deep trouble, and she didn't know what to do about it.

She was heavily perspiring now, and she clenched the steering wheel tightly, trying to stop her hands from shaking as she fought down the rising sense of panic that made it hard for her to think straight. All through her trial, she had maintained her composure in spite of everything that was thrown at her not only on the witness stand but during the intense interrogations that had preceded it. But now was different. Now she was possibly going to be set upon while she had her child to protect. She thought maybe she should phone her grandfather and tell him what was happening to her. But what good would that do? Except to put him on the right track for hunting somebody down after she and Laura were kidnapped or killed.

CHAPTER 34

I drove to Roland's house without letting Joy or Vito know what might be going on. Roland didn't ask me to do it but I felt like I ought to. When Diane asked me where I was going, I mumbled something about taking some paperwork over there. I didn't want to get everyone in an uproar at this stage. Maybe the situation would resolve itself without justifying our worst fears, then Roland and I would be able to breathe a sigh of relief without having to make anyone else sweat it out.

No sooner did I pull into his driveway when he burst out of the house slamming the door. He was wearing a black jacket, black jeans, and black boots, and when he saw me he said, "Go home, Dave. Let me handle this."

"No way. I'm in for the duration."

"Okay, this isn't your first rodeo," he said. "But you better not fold under pressure. We're gonna go in my car." He pressed a button on a remote and made the garage door go up. Then he tugged a pistol out of his belt and handed it to me and said, "Take this. I've got another one in my shoulder holster."

He got behind the wheel of a bright red Buick convertible, one that I hadn't seen before, and I climbed into the passenger seat. "This is a rental," he said. "I hope we don't roll it if we get into a high-speed chase. Put your seat belt on." When he said that, the threat of imminent danger really hit home to me.

He backed out of the garage with the tires squealing, then he hit the gas pretty hard and quickly picked up too much speed for his residential neighborhood.

I asked where we were going.

"Gotta head for Route 30. I told Katherine—I mean Sarah—that a good place for us to hook up would be the Buy-and-Fly a few miles from the Turnpike exit. I don't know if she ever got there or where she might be by now but that's where we should start hunting for her."

The Irwin Turnpike exit was only about a half hour from where Roland and I both lived, if we were traveling at the legal speed limits. But we weren't. I had to warn Roland that if we got hauled in by a cop his chase after Sarah and Laura would be over. Then he slowed down, but not by much, and urgently pounded his horn at anybody who got in front of us. In spite of those kinds of slowdowns, we zoomed through Clairton and McKeesport, hit Route 48 and then onto Route 30 in record time that scared me half out of my wits. It was the way Roland used to drive when we were teenagers—and it used to scare the hell out of my way back then.

It was a partial relief when he swerved into the parking lot of the Buy-and-Fly. I say "partial" because we were there but where the hell was Sarah? Neither she nor her daughter were standing in the bright lights sipping milk shakes. We got out, slamming the doors of the rented Buick' and barged into the place. Out of the few customers standing in a line in front of the clerks, or the two or three who were browsing among the racks, we didn't see any of the people we were looking for. Of course we didn't even have any recent photos to show the two clerks.

But an older gentleman, balding and probably in his forties, came out of a side room, cast a sharp look at us and said half apologetically, "Excuse me, fellers, but you look pretty upset about something. Anything I can help you with?"

Roland said, "We're looking for my granddaughter and her little girl. They were supposed to meet us here."

"I think they *were* here. I'm the manager and I keep an eye out for strange goings-on. Convenience stores are targets for robbers."

Roland pounced on that comment. "Something made you take notice of them? Why?"

"I saw them outside, talking to a guy who pulled up next to them in a black SUV. The lady had pink hair but that's nothing unusual these days. She got into the SUV and left her own car here, without coming in. And when the SUV pulled out of here, the little girl was still in a booster chair in the back seat of her mom's car."

"How'd you know she was the little girl's mom?" Roland said urgently.

"Because I took the little girl out of the booster seat and brought her in here and tried to give her pop and potato chips. But she was bawling too much. So I called the cops and told them I had her here and didn't know who she was. They came and tried to talk with her, then took her to the police station after getting in touch with a social worker. She might still be in police custody. Poor thing."

Roland's face looked more strained than I had ever seen it as he stared at the Buy-and-Fly manager. Then he said, "Give us the best description you can of the lady who went with the guy in the black SUV. And him too."

"I can do better than that," the manager said. "I took down his license plate number."

CHAPTER 35

"Where are we going?" Sarah asked.

But the driver didn't answer. Back at the Buy-and-Fly he had pointed a gun at her and barked at her, "Get the kid and get her in my car, booster seat and all! Right this minute or I'll shoot you both right here in the parking lot!"

Instantly overcome with desperation she said, "*Please*—I'll go with you, but don't take my daughter!"

"You get in the passenger seat and I'll think about it," he said. "Right this second!"

He became more agitated when he spotted two more vehicles pulling in.

She took advantage of his state of mind and got into his SUV in hopes that he would forget about Laura now that other people were starting to stare at him.

It seemed to work because he said nothing more about taking Sarah and Laura both and once Sarah got into the vehicle, he hit the gas.

Now she was doubting the wisdom of the trade-off she had offered while at the same time trying to believe she was lucky to have thought of it in the intense fear that had overwhelmed her at that moment.

She hoped she had saved Laura's life. As with almost any mother, her own life came second. But now she was plagued with worries about what was going to happen to Laura? Maybe somebody would come along and rescue her as soon as they realized she had been abandoned. But maybe not. Sarah's heart tightened and skipped a beat when she pictured her innocent young daughter dying of heat exhaustion in the hot car. It had been a sweltering day for early July, and Sarah had kept the air conditioning on high while she was driving. Now she hoped the evening had cooled down quickly enough that extreme heat wasn't the greatest danger to her daughter.

What would a pedophile do if he found a female child in an unlocked car with the mother nowhere in sight? Sarah shuddered when she thought of that, and her captor snickered at her.

He said, "What's the matter? Are you cold or just scared?"

"Please let me go," she pleaded. "I'll hitchhike back to the Buy-and-Fly."

"Don't worry, you're not *flying* anywhere," he said with a scowl.

She pictured herself dying while hoping that she might have saved Laura. *Might have.* She had no way of knowing. She could only conjecture as she wavered between hope and dread. She was struck by the bitter thought that when she allowed herself to be kidnapped she was only a half hour or so from her grandfather's house. If she had not stopped at the Buy-and-Fly in an attempt to get away from the creep who was following her, who turned out to be *this* creep, she would have arrived at her grandfather's house by now, both she and Laura getting lots of hugs and kisses, warmed in the beginning stages of renewable love. But her attempt to ditch the creep had backfired and caused her to fall into his hands.

"Why didn't you blindfold me?" she asked him.

"So you can enjoy the scenery," he said.

But Sarah knew the real reason. Kirk and his cronies didn't make any bones about it. Many times she had heard them say that if you knew you were ultimately going to kill your hostages, you didn't need to blindfold them or wear a mask in front of them unless you wanted to give them the false hope that you would not harm them so long as they cooperated and played nice.

Sarah could tell that her captor had a smirk on his face even though she was looking at him sideways. He was peering straight through the windshield, which was crystal clear, and so were the tinted windows. His Cadillac SUV was as clean or cleaner than the cars in a showroom. This probably meant he was OCD, Sarah thought, but she had little confidence in her deduction and couldn't see how it could help her. He was outwardly sort of ruggedly good-looking even if his soul was damaged like that of her ex-husband. But his head looked too small for his broad-shouldered narrow-hipped body. At the Buy-and-Fly when he was standing almost right against her sticking his gun in her ribs, she felt like she was facing a seven-foot tall three hundred-pound ogre wearing a black nylon jacket, black trousers, and a wide black belt with an overly large Harley-Davidson buckle. He kept his black pistol in his lap where the likelihood that Sarah could snatch it from him was zero to none.

"Where are you taking me?" she asked him.

"You'll find out, so stop pestering me," he told her.

When they hit Route 51 South and stayed on it for about fifteen miles, then took the ramp onto Route 70, she was pretty sure they were heading toward Little Washington, Kirk's old stomping grounds. A much greater dose of fear overwhelmed her then—because although she still didn't know who her captor was, she figured out *what* he was, then gasped and blurted, "You must've known my husband!"

"Kirk Biggins? Of course."

"Damn you to hell!" Sarah said, giving him the finger.

He laughed at her, then told her, "He was a great man, or he could've been, but you took that away from him."

"He was a traitor and a pervert! You must be one too! Why don't you just kill me *now* and get it over with?"

"Because I have plans for you," he answered smugly. "And you have plans too. The kind of plans that I badly need."

"You mean those stupid bomb building plans," Sarah shot back at him. "Well, I burned them. You can torture me all you want and it won't do you a bit of good because I certainly don't remember any of the details."

"We shall see about that," said her captor.

CHAPTER 36

Luckily Vito Martinelli still had friends in the Clairton Police Department even though he was now a private investigator. He was able to get a late-shift detective to run the license plate number jotted down by the manager of the Buy-and-Fly where Sarah Jamison was abducted and little Sarah was abandoned. Then in short order the detective emailed Vito a photocopy of the driver's license held by a man named Todd Nalepka, and Vito relayed the photocopy to Roland's cell phone. So now we knew what Nalepka looked like plus his date of birth and address.

When Roland saw the address, he said, "Damn! That's in the Little Washington area! It can't be a coincidence. He's got to be tied in with Kirk Biggins or the Aryan Confederacy or both."

"A good possibility," I agreed.

We were sitting in Roland's Buick and still parked in front of the Buy-and-Fly since we had no idea what to do till we got additional information. We were chomping at the bit to go after Nalepka and Sarah before it was too late—but the very next thing that Roland had to do was phone the Irwin Police Department to make sure they knew he was Laura's grandfather and that her mother had been kidnapped. He was assured by a female detective that Child Protective Services was taking good care of Laura and that she couldn't be placed in his care without consent from her mother followed up by approval by CPS.

"We're trying desperately to locate her mother right away," Roland said. "To whom am I speaking, just in case I have to get back in touch with you."

"Detective Rita Maksin. I hope you find Laura's mother soon. Laura is a bright little girl. She told us her own age, her mom's name, Sarah Jamison, and that they came here from their home in Philadelphia. You should fill out a Missing Person Report on the mom so we can get on it. Meantime we'll put out a BOLO on this guy Nalepka as well as Sarah."

"I wish you wouldn't do that just yet," Roland said. "He might panic and kill her and dump her body someplace where we'll never find it."

"We can't sandbag the situation once we know about it," Detective Maksin said. "I'm sorry about that, mister…"

"Fornyay," Roland said, then spelled it for her. "Roland Fornyay. That's how it's pronounced. I'm sure you have my cell phone number on your screen now. Please keep me informed."

"Will do, Mr. Fornier."

He ended the call, turned toward me in reverse to back out, and said, "I hope the snake is headed back to his hole. Nalepka. We don't have anything else to go on so we've gotta go to Little Washington, Dave."

"Don't worry about me, I'm with you all the way," I told him.

My adrenaline was flowing and so was my sense of *deja vu*. There were times when we were young men when we had to do use our fists against guys who accosted us in bars or dance halls. I flashed back to the time down by the river when six punks from McKeesport were about to gang up on us till Roland opened a beer bottle with his teeth and nonchalantly spit the cap out.

They clammed up, and we walked farther up the beach. Then when we saw them climb up a bull rope and into an empty barge, we went back there and Roland cut the barge loose with his six-inch folding knife. And the bull rope that had been anchoring the barge was the same kind of bull rope that we stole in order to build our boxing ring in the woods back when we were teenagers.

Now we were comrades in arms once again, but on a much more desperate level.

CHAPTER 37

Watching the countryside fly past the side window of the black SUV, Sarah was surprised that they sped past Little Washington and kept going for another thirty-some miles on a two-lane blacktop. Once again, she knew the territory from when Kirk was alive. She never thought she'd be back there again, and she hated it and feared being there more than ever in her present circumstances.

When the SUV had been going seventy-plus miles per hour on Interstate 79 she didn't dare to think about opening her door and jumping out, but now that they had slowed to fifty and sometimes even forty or thirty-five, she clenched her teeth and tried to work up the courage to fling her side door open and roll, not jump. But she couldn't stop picturing her skull shattering on the pavement. She remembered the horrible way her classmate's older brother, Norman, was killed on his way to the Meadows casino with a friend of his. Norman was in the passenger seat, just as Sarah was now, when a big deer jumped out in front of them. The driver swerved to try to miss it but smacked into the deer at a very high speed and Norman wasn't wearing his seatbelt and he was ejected onto the highway. Maybe he would've survived in spite of multiple broken bones or other severe injuries—but a pickup truck ran over his head. Sarah had attended Norman's closed-casket funeral, so she hadn't seen his crushed head but she had never been able to free herself of the grisly pictures her mind conjured up whether she was awake or asleep. She would have to overcome those images to make herself brave enough to jump out of a moving car. She started inching her hand a bit closer to the lock button near the armrest. Little by little, she got to where the button was almost in reach of the tip of her index finger and that's when her captor snickered at her.

"Cut that out," he warned her. "I've been watching you out of the corner of my eye. You ought to be glad, too. If you work up the nerve to jump out, you'll either kill yourself or I'll do it for you and your little girl will grow up without a mommy."

"You're going to kill me anyway," she said dismally.

"Not if you give me everything I want."

"Sex!" she jeered at him. "Are you one of these jerks who can't get a girlfriend?"

"Don't worry, I get plenty," he shot back at her. "Don't think I'm like that poor twerp in Los Angeles who started strangling the girls he went to high school with because they wouldn't go to bed with him. He didn't have the guts to just take what he needed. But he lost his nerve after he only killed two of them, then he sat in his car and shot himself in the head."

"That's what you ought to do right now!" Sarah snapped.

"You don't really mean that. Hate often turns to love, you know. That's what's going to happen between you and me. I can be your little girl's stepdaddy. I've got plenty of money. I'll take good care of you both."

"Shove your money up your ass, freako!"

"Be careful what you say to me because I'm in total control here. Your grandfather can't help you. I know every move he's going to make. I've had his house bugged for days."

"So what! He's smarter than you are. He's gonna find you and kill you."

"Dream on, babe. But I'll make you a deal. You be real nice to me and I won't kill your daughter after I kill you. *If* I kill you, which I haven't made up my mind yet. But I'll know where to seek out your daughter because if you should end up dead, Roland will take her in, I'm sure of it."

Sarah hadn't been quite sure of it, but she was now for some reason, and it gave her a degree of comfort even in her misery.

CHAPTER 38

Roland and I had no way of knowing that we were taking a different route toward Washington, Pennsylvania, than the kidnapper was on. He was traveling by means of Interstate 376 through Pittsburgh proper and then onto Interstate 79 while we had taken Route 51 South and then the ramp onto Route 70 South. Our objective was Todd Nalepka's condo because that was the address on his driver's license. We realized he might not be going there, but we had to take a chance because it was the only option we had.

While we were speeding in that direction, Roland handed his cell phone to me and told me to call Sheriff Boyce and tell him what had happened and what we were doing about it. I thought this was a wise move plus an indication that Roland wasn't intent on killing Nalepka if we caught up with him. Surely he wouldn't have wanted the sheriff to interfere by putting him in handcuffs either before or after he took the law into his own hands.

I gave his cell phone back to him and said, "I'll use mine. I have the sheriff in my contact list. It's way after normal hours so he might not be in his office, but I'll try."

"Well, *somebody* will be there who will know how to reach him whether he's at a bowling alley or having dinner with his wife. Give it a try, old buddy."

I was about to do that when my cell phone buzzed. It was Vito. He said, "Joy and I don't have anything new for you, we're just worried like hell so I'm calling to make sure you're all right. I have you on speakerphone so Joy can hear you. We didn't want to shake Diane up, so we didn't clue her in yet."

"Thanks, you did right," I said. "We found out who the kidnapper is, thanks to a witness who got his license number. He's a guy named Todd Nalepka, and his address is in the vicinity of Little Washington—what a coincidence, huh?"

"You took the words right out of my mouth. Be safe. Let us know what's happening."

Joy said, "Take care, Dad. We're holding down the fort in case you need us. We're not going to leave till you say we can."

Vito said, "I wish I was with Roland instead of you, Dave. You're just a civilian. Don't take any crazy chances."

"You don't have to tell me that. I'm not out to be a hero."

"Goodbye for now then. Don't take any crazy chances," he repeated.

The handgun Roland had given me was in the pocket of my jacket and I could feel its weight and its outline. I was pretty sure I'd be able to pull the trigger on someone if I had to. I had steeled myself to do so on other cases we had worked on which had put me in considerable danger, but so far, I hadn't actually shot anybody. Usually the only guns I handled were movie props, and I was extra careful when I had to have my actors fire blanks because I knew of two famous young actors who had died in gun accidents, Jon Eric Hexum and Brandon Lee, who was

shot in the abdomen not by a live bullet but by what's called a dumdum, which is a fake head of a bullet. They have to be inserted into the cylinder of a revolver so that, in head-on shots, the audience won't see empty chambers. Somebody forgot to remove one of the dumdums and when a blank was fired it powered the dumdum right into Brandon Lee's body.

In spite of the kinds of movies I made, I was always greatly in favor of nonviolence in real life. I was appalled by the mayhem in our communities, especially the mass shootings of school children. I believed strongly that the ban against civilians being able to acquire weapons of war like AR-15s should be reinstituted. Even when it came to one-on-one crimes, I wanted those who chose to commit them, especially repeat offenders, to get much stiffer penalties. But we were living in a weak-minded society that didn't have the guts to protect itself against child molesters but turned them loose by the dozens as registered sex offenders. Every time a child fell victim to one of them, it was discovered that a hundred or more were living within a five-mile radius of the child's home or school.

I cried when I saw on the evening news that a five-year-old girl in Florida was raped and strangled by a forty-five-year-old man who got convicted and sentenced to death mainly because the child's DNA was found on the armrest of his pickup truck— and the lab technician who had done the analysis testified that the DNA came from her tears.

What could be sadder than that? And it happens over and over. Another little girl in Florida was kept by her demented captor in a closet for two weeks and when he got too scared of being found out, he buried her alive with her teddy bear.

I knew that Kirk Gibbins, in addition to being a neo-Nazi, was also a pedophile, but at this point I was unaware that Todd Nalepka was one too. I intended to ask Sheriff Boyce to run Nalepka's name and DOB—date of birth—through the system to find out if he had a rap sheet, but when I activated the sheriff's number on my phone and hit "call" I got an electronic voice.

"I'm hearing that his message box is full," I told Roland.

This irritated him and he snapped at me, "Call Sheriff Boyce's office—*somebody* will answer. We have to get him to run a BOLO on this fucked-up creep, Todd Nalepka."

"Okay, okay," I said. "I have to dial Information."

"Get on it," Roland told me, treating me like an underling, but I didn't get mad because I realized that's what I was.

CHAPTER 39

Unbeknownst to me and Roland, Todd Nalepka was backing his pickup truck out of a storage unit after forcing Sarah at gunpoint to get into the passenger seat. He had already pulled his Escalade into an adjacent storage unit. We found out later that he owned the entire bank of units, thirty-six of them, under an assumed name. He used a remote to make both doors go down, then got behind the steering wheel of the pickup, congratulating himself that a BOLO wouldn't find him if they were looking for a black Cadillac Escalade.

"Where are we going now?" Sarah asked.

"Curiosity killed the cat."

"How original," she scoffed.

"You're so feisty; you're gonna be fun to fuck," he told her.

It was almost totally dark now, and her scattered and futile thoughts of escaping were fading away.

About ten miles later, Nalepka made a right turn onto a narrow dirt road that he drove on for several additional miles, till he pulled the pickup into a field in the middle of nowhere. At first it looked to Sarah as if nothing was there, but then the headlight beams fell upon a ten-foot-high chain-link fence topped with razor wire, and behind the fence she saw a trailer and a steel shed. As her captor pulled closer, a motion sensor must have been activated because bright lights came on, illuminating the fenced-in area.

Nalepka pulled his pickup close to the chain-links and said, "I have to get out and undo the lock. Don't try to jump out and run toward the woods because I'll shoot you, maybe just in your legs, but maybe not. Depends on how mad you make me. Remember, I'm a dead shot."

Once he had the gate open, he got back behind the wheel and pulled the pickup inside the fence, parking it behind the trailer where it couldn't be easily seen even if somebody came looking. Then he ordered Sarah to get out and with his gun held on her once again he marched her toward the storage shed and mockingly performed a half bow to beckon her in.

But she balked, then faced him. "You're going to keep me in *there?*" she stammered.

"You won't be locked up for long and it's comfy enough," he told her. "I had one of my pretty young girls in there for over two weeks. Till I got tired of her."

"And then you killed her, I guess."

"That's for me to know and you to wonder."

"Go fuck yourself, you asshole!"

He didn't flinch. Instead he said, "Why should I do that when I have you?"

She stuck her tongue out and gave him the raspberries.

He said, "I see you've got a mean and nasty side to you, to go along with your feistiness. Tomorrow morning you'll see how nice I can be in spite of how badly you've been treating me. I'm going to take you to a place that has a totally delicious big breakfast on the menu. It's even called The Big Breakfast. We we'll enjoy a fine meal to start our day, then we'll come back here and get down to our main business."

"Which will be torturing me, I suppose," she said dismally. "My ex-husband was a sadist too so I know all too well how they operate. Kirk would beat me or rape me, then he'd buy me roses. That's why I made him my ex."

"No, I'm not at all like that," Nalepka said with a touch of self-pity. "You do me an injustice, Kathleen."

She was stunned to hear her birth name coming out of his mouth. But she said nothing.

He went on as if still feeling sorry for himself. "I'm really hoping you won't make me hurt you. I'm not that kind of guy. If you just give me what I want, I'll make you as free as a bird."

Then suddenly he lunged at Sarah, grabbed her by her slender throat and started choking the life out of her. She clawed at his hands with no effect whatsoever and felt herself passing out. But he let loose of her just as suddenly as he had pounced, and she almost fell to the floor but struggled to retain her balance.

He laughed demonically. "If you don't play nice tomorrow, remember that no one can hear you scream. I'm going to start slicing off little chunks of you, starting down at your ankles and working my way upward slowly…ever so slowly until you beg me to kill you, but of course I won't. I'll just keep on cutting off pieces until you tell me where Kirk's documents are."

"I told you, they're useless to you!"

"Well, I don't believe you. I want to see for myself."

Trembling, not wanting to look into his face any longer, she backed away from him, into the shed, and then he shut the steel door and locked her inside. She heard the metallic sounds made by the lock and the keeper, not nearly as loud as the clanging shut of a door to a prison cell, but just as frightening.

At least she was alone and he wasn't any longer an immediate threat.

To her surprise, a night light came on inside the eight-by-ten steel encasement and a fan started blowing. The feel of the sudden air flow made her turn her head and spot the rotating fan on top of a wooden crate, next to a six-foot by three-foot lawn chair cushion obviously meant for her to sleep on. She realized that the paltry creature comforts that Mr. Freako had provided were meant to keep her alive live till morning instead of letting her die from heat stroke during the hot, humid night.

A fit of pure rage suddenly overwhelmed her, and she pounded and kicked at the steel door as hard as she could, with hot salty tears streaming down her face, picturing herself battering her captor's face yet knowing all the while that nothing she did would break the lock on the other side of the steel door and make it sag open.

Exhausted, she flopped down onto the long, flowery, plastic-covered chair cushion and cried and cried till she sank into a fitful sleep. She dreamed that her arms and legs were tired to the point of near death from carrying Laura up a steep hill that seemed to never end and to have such an unfathomable height to it that its top could never be reached.

CHAPTER 40

Roland and I were less than five miles from Todd Nalepka's condo when Sheriff Boyce finally called me back. When I heard his voice, I put him on speakerphone.

"Where are you?" he barked, making me feel like I was going to be reprimanded for some reason.

"Pretty close to Nalepka's condo," I answered calmly.

"Well, don't go there. CSI is there ahead of you and Nalepka isn't there I got a tip from a bouncer at a biker bar called The Kick Stand who says Nalepka hangs out there and thinks he's in with the in crowd, but they think he's just a wannabe and a closet gay who thinks he's better than they are, so none of them minded ratting him out."

"Ratting him out how?" Roland asked right away.

"The bouncer's uncle mows grass part-time for Nalepka at a defunct farm the asshole owns. The bikers believe that he cooks meth there in a trailer because he always has some to give out. Apparently, he kisses their asses to buddy up to them. Acts macho but secretly wants to blow them."."

"Where's the defunct farm?" Roland sharply interjected. "I think I should be on hand when my granddaughter gets rescued. She's going to be traumatized. She has PTSD and I've always been able to get her calmed down. I'm sure I'll need to take her to a therapist after all this is over. It's a shame it had to happen just when she was doing so well, holding down a full-time job and being a good mother."

Roland was lying of course. He had no idea if his granddaughter had PTSD or any other mental disorder, but obviously thought it to be a good angle to play in the heat of the moment, and it worked because Sheriff Boyce hemmed and hawed at first but ended up telling us how to find our way to Nalepka's secret acreage and said it would take us at least twenty minutes to get there. "Don't hurry," he told us. "There's nothing you can do and nothing we can't handle. Just don't try to interfere."

By the time we spotted the fenced-in trailer and steel cage Sheriff Boyce and his deputies were already on the scene with pistols, shotguns and assault weapons pointed right at the trailer's side door. The night was darker now but bright lights had come on. The gate was hanging open on just one of its hinges and parts of the chain-link fence had been cut away with shears or a blowtorch and parts of it bulldozed over.

The sheriff glanced at me and Roland, shaking his head in disdain as we got out of the red Buick. Roland drew his pistol and motioned for me to do the same so I pulled the one he had given me out of my jacket pocket, wondering if Sheriff Boyce was going to let me keep it.

"Get the fuck outta here or stand back!" he yelled.

Roland yelled back, "I'm licensed to carry, but David isn't! Put your weapon away, Dave!"

I was actually glad to hear him say that. I didn't want to have to shoot anybody, and with the sheriff and his deputies on the scene I didn't see why I would need to.

"I'm commanding you to put your pistol away and stand way back!" the sheriff shouted at Roland. "If you don't obey I'll put you in cuffs!"

Roland finally gave in, but he didn't look happy about it and I didn't need to see the scowl on his face in order to imagine his anger and disappointment. The chance of killing Todd Nalepka was slipping away from him. He likely had been wishing that he could goad Nalepka into coming out of that trailer with a weapon in his hand and Sarah in front of him as a shield, which to

Nalepka's surprise would not have stopped Roland from firing his Glock. I knew what kind of a marksman Roland was from our teenage days of shooting rats with his lever-action .22 rifle down at the city dump in Clairton. He would have killed Nalepka with an expertly placed bullet in the forehead and eventually he probably would've gotten a complete exoneration even if he had to go through interrogation after interrogation along the way. But much as he might have wished for it, now it wasn't going to happen, and he and I retreated to a position just inside the wreckage of the chain-link fence.

Sheriff Boyce glanced back at us to make sure we had complied. Then he raised a handheld megaphone to his lips.

Todd Nalepka! Come out with your hands up! This is Sheriff Boyce! We have you outnumbered! Come out with your hands up!"

Not a sound came from inside the trailer, but all of a sudden there was banging and yelling coming from the steel shed.

The sheriff and two or three of his deputies took their eyes off of the trailer long enough to look toward the shed, and Roland and I did too, while most of the deputies, male and female, resolutely kept their weapons pointed just as they had been.

There was more banging and yelling from inside the shed but Sheriff Boyce didn't flinch. He yelled, "Hold your positions! Hold your positions! Don't lose focus!" Then, using his megaphone and presuming that Todd Nalepka was holed up in the trailer even though there was no response from in there, the sheriff blasted out another demand.

"Todd Nalepka! Come out with your hands up! This is your final warning!"

Like everyone else, Roland and I steadfastly stared at the trailer and all the weapons pointed at it. I had put my gun away but Roland had not, which made me even more nervous. I saw his Glock hanging down by his right side with his hip sort of hiding it. I knew he was a good enough shot to have a chance of taking Nalepka down even at this distance, which was about fifty or sixty feet.

The banging and yelling from inside the steel shed had stopped now.

The entire compound was bathed in silence.

Todd Nalepka still hadn't made an appearance. A slew of weapons still pointed at the trailer.

Then there was a scraping sound and the trailer door inched open.

Nalepka came out slowly, holding his hands above his head.

"Don't shoot me! Please don't shoot me! I'm giving up!"

Sheriff Boyce yelled for him to get down on the ground and he immediately complied and was promptly handcuffed, then yanked to his feet.

Roland and I then ran up to the shed even though the sheriff yelled, "Get back here!"

But we didn't stop—because the banging from inside the shed had resumed.

Roland took aim and shot the lock off.

And then Sarah came out and fell into his arms.

They were both crying and my own face was also wet with tears.

CHAPTER 41

Like all malignant narcissists, Todd Nalepka was so much in love with the limelight he didn't even ask for a percentage of the royalties from this book when he allowed me to interview him in the Washington County jail. Perhaps he already knew he wouldn't be permitted to keep the money anyway because there's a law forbidding criminals from profiting from their crimes.

He told me about as many of his victims as he could remember, thirteen in all, but he said there were probably more that he must have forgotten. I don't doubt that it's true.

Roland's granddaughter, Sarah, as she's now known, underwent considerable trauma by telling me all the things that she was subjected to that Roland and I had no way of knowing till she revealed them. She didn't want to be paid anything, but I gave her a Letter of Agreement stating that she will receive fifty percent of my royalties for this book. She has told me she will put any money that comes to her in a trust fund for Laura that she can claim when she turns eighteen. That will ensure that she can go to the college of her choice. If she happens to be awarded a scholarship, the money will still be hers.

Sarah and Laura reside in Fort Lauderdale now, where Roland and Jocko are still hunting sunken galleons and having seagoing adventures. Lauderdale is a wonderful part of America for my little family—Diane and Joy and I, often joined by Vito and Donna—to visit on vacations, and I often make excuses to go there to spend time with Roland and not lose track of him as I had previously done for twenty years. I don't think he and

Jocko have killed anyone lately. Or possibly ever, for all I really know.

After Todd Nalepka took a plea deal of life without parole in return for telling where the remains of his victims were buried and for the death penalty to be taken off the table, he was convicted and sentenced to a federal prison in West Virginia where he did not last long even though federal prisons were supposed to be safer for convicts than the non-federal ones. This may be so, for all I know, but it didn't prove so for Todd. He only served nine months before being beaten and shanked, and so far no one has been punished for it and I don't think that anyone ever will be. No surprise. The same thing happened to Jeffrey Dahmer and Stanley Haas, and with the same result in that the person or persons who killed them never got found out.

I often thought about the Stanley Haas case because I was only fourteen when it happened, and it was in the days when grisly murders were so rare that they made headlines for days and days. Haas escaped from the Pennsylvania prison and kidnapped a beautiful young woman and her nine-month-old baby and kept them as hostages. Then when things got too hot for him and having a frightened woman and a baby in her car with him while he was driving it was too likely to catch a cop's attention, he put the baby in a cardboard box and shot it full of holes, then he raped and killed the young mother.

When my mother and I read about it in the *Pittsburgh Press,* she said, "I think if they catch him, they should tie him to a tree and let whoever who wants to go up and drive one nail in him."

It was the only time I ever heard my mom talk that way.

"Would you want to?" I asked her.

She said, "I don't know, maybe I would."

Just a few years ago, I met an old man in a bar who told me he was in a prison guard where the baby killer, Stanley Haas, was locked up after he got caught and drew a life sentence. "We made sure he didn't last long," the old man said. "We put him in a cell block where a lot of the inmates didn't like guys like him. He lasted two months before they choked him to death, same as he done to the baby's mother. They done it in the movie room of the prison after the movie came on and the seats were dark enough that they could get away with it."

During the whole time that Stanley Haas was on the loose, I felt the way my mother did.

And now that Todd Alepka was gone, I wasn't going to shed any tears over him. Instead, I was happy that Roland's granddaughter and her little girl wouldn't have to keep looking over their shoulders.

Alepka never knew it but if he *had* succeeded in torturing Sarah until she gave him the key to her locker in the YWCA, where she made him believe she had stashed plans for a dirty bomb, he would have found that it contained nothing but gym clothes.

For more information on John Russo,
his books, movies, and official merchandise,
please visit:

www.TheJohnRusso.com

ABOUT THE AUTHOR

With 40 books published internationally and 19 movies in worldwide distribution, John Russo has been called "a Living Legend." He began by co-authoring the screenplay for the horror classic, *Night of the Living Dead*, and went on to build an iconic decades-long career.

His books on the art and craft of movie making have become bibles of independent production and have won a national award for Superior Nonfiction. Quentin Tarantino and many other noted filmmakers have stated that Russo's books have helped them launch their careers.

John Russo wants people to know he's "just a nice guy who likes to scare people" -- and he's done it with novels and films such as *Return of the Living Dead, Midnight, The Majorettes, The Awakening, Heartstopper,* and *My Uncle John is a Zombie!*

He's had a long, rewarding career, and he shows no signs of slowing down. In 2024, Lionsgate acquired a Western written by him, *The Night They Came Home*, about the murder spree perpetrated by the Rufus Buck gang, who were all hanged in 1895.

Russo's popularity among genre fans remains at a high pitch. He appears at many movie conventions each year as a featured guest, and hundreds of attendees come to his tables or to the bar to share drinks, jokes, and serious conversation.